THE SUMMER WE SAVED THE BEES

Robin Stevenson

ORCA BOOK PUBLISHERS

Library and Archives Canada Cataloguing in Publication

Stevenson, Robin, 1968–, author
The summer we saved the bees / Robin Stevenson.

Issued in print and electronic formats.
ISBN 978-1-4598-0834-8 (pbk.).—ISBN 978-1-4598-0835-5 (pdf).—
ISBN 978-1-4598-0836-2 (epub)

I. Title.
PS8637.T487S94 2015   jc813'.6   C2015-901702-5
C2015-901703-3

First published in the United States, 2015
Library of Congress Control Number: 2015935535

Summary: In this middle-grade novel, twelve-year-old Wolf's mother is obsessed
with saving the world's honeybees, but Wolf is less than enthusiastic about her plan
to take her bee activism on the road.

*Orca Book Publishers is dedicated to preserving the environment and
has printed this book on Forest Stewardship Council® certified paper.*

Orca Book Publishers gratefully acknowledges the support for its publishing programs
provided by the following agencies: the Government of Canada through the Canada Book
Fund and the Canada Council for the Arts, and the Province of British Columbia
through the BC Arts Council and the Book Publishing Tax Credit.

Cover design by Teresa Bubela
Cover images by iStockphoto.com
Author photo by Sushi Rice Studios

ORCA BOOK PUBLISHERS
www.orcabook.com

Printed and bound in Canada.

18 17 16 15 • 4 3 2 1

For Amy Mathers, with great respect and appreciation for her Marathon of Books.

One

MOM WAS SEWING when the twins and I left for school in the morning, and she was still sewing when we got home that afternoon. The floor around her was strewn with scraps of yellow lace and black velvet. The electric hum of her sewing machine sounded like the buzz of bees.

Saffron dropped her schoolbag on the hardwood floor with a heavy *thunk*. "Are they done, Mama? Can we see them? Can I try mine on?"

Whisper clutched my hand tightly and said nothing.

"Almost done, kittens." Mom scooped up Saffron and pulled her onto her lap. "Whisper, my love, come give Mama a hug."

Whisper let go of my hand, crept up beside Saffron and leaned her head against Mom's shoulder.

"After dinner you can try them on," Mom said. "I just have to finish the wings."

"And then we can fly!" Saffron shouted.

"And then you can fly," Mom agreed.

Whisper looked at me, and a tiny smile lifted one corner of her mouth.

"I'm hungry," Saffron said, wriggling free.

"Me too," I told her.

Since I'd turned twelve a couple of months ago, I'd been hungry all the time. Like some switch had turned on and no matter how much I ate, it wouldn't turn off. I could eat nonstop and still feel hungry. My stomach was getting pudgy and my jeans were too tight, but I had this gnawing emptiness in my belly that wouldn't go away.

"Violet's making dinner," Mom said, nodding toward the kitchen. "Wolf, why don't you give her a hand? Saffron, you and Whisper can help me sew your wings."

In the kitchen, Violet was chopping huge quantities of tomatoes and onions.

"What are you making?" I asked.

"Chili." She nodded toward a jumbo can of kidney beans. "Open that and rinse them."

I looked at her more closely. Her black eyeliner was smudged, and her eyes were glittering. "Violet? Are you crying?"

She scowled at me. "It's the onions."

I didn't believe her, but I opened the can of beans and said nothing. Probably she'd had another fight with Tyler. Violet thought about nothing but her boyfriend, even though they argued and broke up all the time. When she wasn't fighting *with* Tyler, she was fighting with Mom and Curtis *about* Tyler. I was tired of hearing about him.

Violet sniffed, wiped her nose on her sleeve and swept the chopped onions into the saucepan on the stove. They sizzled in the hot oil. I dumped the beans into a colander and ran cold tap water over them.

"Use a bowl," she said. "You're wasting water."

"Not much." I turned the tap off. "There you go."

She poked the beans with her finger. "Still slimy."

"They're fine." I hooked my thumbs into my pockets. "What's the matter, Vi?"

"It's Jade," she said. "Stupid Jade. I hate her."

Jade is my mom. Her boyfriend, Curtis, is Vi's dad, so Vi is technically my stepsister, or she would be if Curtis and Mom were married. The twins were born after Mom and Curtis met, so they're like the glue that sticks us all together and makes us one family. At least, *I* think of us as a family. It's hard to know what Violet thinks because pretty much everything makes her mad.

"What happened?" I said. "Did you guys have a fight or something?"

She stirred the onions and turned down the burner. "She says Ty can't come with us."

"Where?"

"On the trip, stupid. This summer."

"Oh." I hadn't known Violet wanted Tyler to come, but maybe I should have guessed. "Would his parents let him anyway?"

"He doesn't have to ask them, Wolf. He's seventeen. He can do what he likes."

I nodded. Secretly, I was glad Mom had said no. I didn't really want Ty around when I was dressed as a bee. It was going to be bad enough with strangers staring at us, but at least I'd never have to see them again. We'd just be passing through.

"I bet he'll find some other girl," Violet said. "If we're gone for months and months."

"Maybe you'll find some other guy," I said.

"As if. I'll still be Ty's girlfriend, doofus."

I wondered if she was right. Loving someone doesn't mean you own them, Mom says. She figures that's where most people go wrong—getting loving and owning all mixed up. She says you have to hold love as gently as a baby bird or you'll crush it. *What if it flies away?* Saffron asked once. Mom sighed. *It happens*, she said, and I wondered if she was thinking about my father. He left when I was a baby, and he never came back.

There was a shriek from the living room, and I could hear Mom shouting at the twins to "cut it out right now!" Mom didn't yell much, but when she did, it made you feel like you had to do something right away. Like you had to fix things. "Maybe I should take Whisper and Saffron outside," I said. "Get them out of Mom's hair. She really wants to get the costumes done tonight."

"I don't see what the big rush is," Violet said. She poured the beans into the saucepan with the onions, added the tomatoes and dumped half a jar of chili powder on top of it all. "There's still six weeks left before school finishes."

I shrugged.

"This whole trip is the lamest idea ever." She grabbed a wooden spoon and stirred the chili so violently that a few beans went flying. "And there's no way I'm getting dressed up as a bee or taking part in any kind of presentation or guerrilla theater or whatever kind of hell Jade's planning."

She sounded fierce. Time to leave. I backed out of the kitchen and joined the others. Whatever the problem had been with the twins, they seemed to have figured it out. And it looked like the costumes were pretty much finished. Whisper and Saffron were fluttering around the living room, a blur of yellow and black, wire-and-lace wings dangling limply from their skinny shoulders. Mom clapped and laughed. "Don't they look sweet? My little honeybees."

I watched them for a minute, buzzing this way and that, Saffron climbing up on the back of the couch—"Watch me fly!"—and jumping off, Whisper hugging herself, lost in gales of helpless giggles.

"Wolf," Mom said, and her tone was suddenly serious, "the girls don't know yet, but we're going to leave a little earlier than we'd planned."

"What do you mean?"

"The website's getting lots of traffic. The costumes and signs are done. Curtis has finished converting the van, and it's running great." She lowered her voice. "I think we could be ready to go in a few days. Maybe even by Monday."

Monday was only three days away. I stared at her. "What about school?"

"It won't matter if you miss a few weeks. Besides, traveling's very educational, Wolf. You'll learn more on the road than you ever could in a classroom."

"Mom. School's important."

"So you can homeschool. You've done it before."

I didn't go to school at all until fourth grade, because before that we were living on this tiny island called Lasqueti. It wasn't like I really *homeschooled* though. I just helped Mom with the cabin and the garden and the chickens. I didn't do lessons or anything. Still, when I finally started school, I wasn't behind at all. I could read and write and do everything the other kids could do. I liked to think that meant I was smart, but Mom said it just showed that school was overrated and that counting chicken eggs taught you how to add and subtract just as well as worksheets did. "How can I homeschool?" I asked. "We won't even be at home."

"Roadschool then." She laughed. "Lighten up, Wolf."

I tried to smile, like it was no big deal, but I didn't want to leave early. I loved my school, even though Violet, who went to the regular high school, said it was for losers. There were only about twenty students, including the twins and me. We had a garden, and we got to learn what we wanted, and all the kids did stuff together, not like ordinary schools where you are split up by age. Well, we sort of were—but just into two classes, one for little kids and one for age ten and up. The little kids mostly played, and my group did passion projects, which meant we picked a topic we were interested in, learned about it however we wanted and then presented it to the rest of the group. It didn't have to be a speech or an essay or anything. One older boy was making Haida art, carving orcas and eagles from red cedar. And Caitlin, who was my age and mean to everyone, made dioramas, which sounds dorky but they were actually cool.

For my project, I made a website about bees.

That was actually how all of this started, as Violet reminded me on a daily basis.

"*This whole trip is your fault, Wolf. It's all because of your stupid project. You're the one that got Jade freaked out about the bees dying.*"

"*But before my bee project, she was freaked out about climate change,*" I'd reminded Violet. "*Remember that? And your dad was too, at least as much as Mom.*"

Violet had scowled at me. "*Yeah, well, they never dragged us across the country and made us dress up as melting polar ice, did they?*"

Violet was going to go berserk when she heard we were leaving early. She didn't want to go at all, ever. "I don't want to miss the rest of the year," I told Mom.

She ruffled my hair. "I know, love. But this is important." She put one finger under my chin and lifted it so that I had to look right at her. "This is more important than anything, right?"

"I guess. I mean, yeah." I pulled away, turning my head and avoiding her eyes. "But we're already doing a lot."

We did more than anyone else I knew. We recycled and reused, we grew our own fruit and vegetables, we rode bikes everywhere. We'd never owned a car before the van, and I'd never flown in a plane. When we lived on Lasqueti, we didn't even have electricity until Mom moved in with Curtis, who had solar panels. Before we moved to the city, I thought composting toilets were the norm. And none of us ate meat, except me, once. It was on pizza at another kid's house, and it was sort of an accident.

"I know it's hard," Mom said. "But Wolf, when you're facing a crisis, a life-or-death emergency…you have to think about the big picture. You have to rethink your priorities."

"Yeah. I know."

"We're all going to have to make some sacrifices," she said. "Set aside our comforts and our concerns about what other people might think."

"I just don't see how waiting six weeks would make a difference."

"Don't you?"

I squirmed. I knew what she was going to say before she said it.

"How many bees die each year?" she asked.

"Millions?"

"Yes. About thirty percent of all the bee colonies in the States die," she said. "Every year. And what percentage of our crops is pollinated by bees?"

"About a third?"

She nodded. "Right. And what's our government doing?"

"Nothing?"

She snorted. "A so-called study. Which has been going on for a decade. Meanwhile they're still spraying poison and the clock is counting down, Wolf. We don't know how much time we have."

There was a lump in my throat, and it ached like I'd swallowed some of that poison myself. Mom was right. It was stupid to fuss about school. *Suck it up, buttercup,* like Curtis always said. "I know," I said. "You're right. It'll be fine. Will I get to say goodbye to everyone?"

"Of course. You can go to school Monday and say goodbye." She pulled me close and hugged me tightly. "My brave boy."

"I'm not brave."

"Yes, you are," she said. "Braver than you think."

I hoped so. Because if Mom was right about the world going down the toilet, I was going to need to be.

We all were.

There was a lump in my throat...

I checked Mom's website that night, but she hadn't updated it to say when we were leaving. I looked at the photo of our family, all standing together in the backyard: Mom and Curtis smiling, with their arms around each other's shoulders; me standing behind Whisper and Saffron, my stupid red hair sticking out in every direction. The twins looked cute. I looked like a dork. Violet was standing a little off to one side, like she didn't want to be associated with the rest of us, which was pretty much how she always acted.

I read my mother's words on the home page even though I practically knew them by heart:

My name is Jade Everett and I am sharing my story here in the hope that it might inspire others to join us in our fight.

9

I've always been an activist. For years, I went to protests, I wrote letters, I lived off the grid, trying to reduce our environmental footprint—but I knew I wasn't doing enough. Every day I looked at my children and I imagined their future and I wanted to cry. The polar ice was melting, the reefs were dying, water levels were rising. Our world was dying all around us. ·

I realized years ago that it made no sense to continue our day-to-day life, but I didn't know what to do. It was my son, Wolf, who gave me the idea. He was doing a school project on bee-colony collapse. I realized that the bees were like the canary in the coal mine—and reading about what was happening to them was like seeing the future unfolding. Crop failure. Worldwide food shortages. Famine. Death. Maybe in the next decade! I may never see my children reach adulthood, but at least in these last doomed years my family can try to live in a way that we can be proud of.

And so we will cross the country, traveling from west coast to east coast, stopping at towns along the way to raise awareness of bees and their importance, of the dangers of fungicides and pesticides, of the danger to our food supply if the bees are lost. To show people a glimpse of the future we are barreling toward, and to persuade them to join us in our fight.

To do everything we can to save the bees—and our planet.

Every time I read it, my stomach felt funny, and I got a weird kind of electric tingle down my arms, sort of like when you bang your funny bone really hard.

I wished she hadn't put that part in about it being my idea.

TWO

ON SATURDAY MORNING we were eating breakfast in the kitchen when we heard a horn honking loudly: *bwahh, bwahh, bwahh!* We rushed outside and there was the van, parked in our gravel driveway.

It was white and a little banged up, and it looked like something a plumber would drive, with doors at the back instead of the sides.

Curtis got out and stood there with his arms spread wide. His dark hair hung almost to his shoulders, his jeans were streaked with blackish grease, and he hadn't shaved in a few days. His chin was right on the line between stubble and beard, hundreds of short hairs glinting in the bright sunlight. "Well, gang? What do you think?"

"Can I paint it?" Saffron asked.

"Sure you can. You all can."

Whisper looked at me, her bottom lip sticking out. Violet raised her eyebrows. "A Ford? Seriously? You bought a *Ford*?"

"Wait till you see inside," Curtis said, beckoning to us. He was grinning, his dark eyes crinkled into shiny crescents and his teeth gleaming white. We all headed over to the van and waited as he threw open the back doors. A foam mattress took up most of the cargo area. Curtis lifted one corner and rapped his knuckles on the plywood beneath it. "Plenty of storage under there," he said.

"Whose bed is it?" Saffron asked him.

"Me and your mom's."

Jade stroked Saffron's hair. "You girls can sleep with us if you want to, or in the tent with Violet and Wolf. You might like to be with the big kids."

Whisper climbed onto the mattress and curled up like a kitten in the sun. I looked past her at the two rows of seats, the propane stove and the icebox, and tried to imagine this being our home.

"What about all our stuff?" Violet asked.

"We'll get rid of most of it," Mom said. "And we've rented a storage locker for the things we decide to keep."

Violet curled her lip. "It smells like French fries."

Curtis grinned. "We're running on 100 percent vegetable oil, baby."

Mom flung her arms around him, and he lifted her and swung her around so her long red hair flew out behind her like flames. Then he put her down and kissed her.

"Gross," Violet said. It wasn't clear whether she meant the French-fry smell or the kissing.

"Can we paint it now?" Saffron asked.

Curtis released my mom. "Have to get you some paint first."

"Today?"

"This weekend, yeah. If we're gonna head out next week, we've got to get busy."

Violet stared at him. "Excuse me? *Excuse* me? If we're going to do *what*?"

Mom looked at Curtis. "I haven't talked to her about our change in plans. I thought perhaps you should do that."

Curtis ran his hands through his hair and turned to Violet, who was glaring at him through eyes narrowed to slits. "So Violet," he began, "the thing is, we're ready to go, right? And so why bother paying rent for June if we could just move out?"

"Um, maybe because you promised I could finish the year, Dad. And school goes until the end of June."

Curtis shrugged. "I'm sure your teachers will understand."

"Yeah? Well, I'm pretty sure they won't, Dad." Violet's eyebrows were drawn together, and as she waited for him to reply, she pressed her lips together so hard they turned almost white. Curtis gestured helplessly, lifting his hands and letting them drop back to his sides, and Violet shot him a look of pure loathing. "Anyway, I don't care when you're leaving," she said. "I'm not going unless Ty can come."

"I want Ty to come too," Saffron said.

"There aren't enough seat belts," Mom said.

Violet swung around and turned on her, letting loose a whole stream of words she wasn't allowed to say in front of the twins. I put my hands over Saffron's ears.

Mom looked at me. "Take the girls in the house, would you, Wolf?"

13

I nodded. "Come on, Whisper. Let's plan how to paint the van, okay?"

Whisper hopped down and took my hand. I tried to listen to what Curtis was saying to Violet, but his voice was so low I couldn't quite make it out. Something about money and rent and him getting flak from someone.

"Yellow," Saffron said, skipping toward the house. "With black stripes, like a bee."

"No way," I said. "No way am I driving around in—"

Whisper's grip on my hand tightened. "Like a bee," she breathed, so quietly I barely heard her.

I looked down at her wide brown eyes and sighed. "Really? You guys want to drive across the country in a van that looks like a giant bee?"

They nodded in unison. "With wings," Saffron said.

In the house, I found paper and markers, and the girls started drawing pictures of bee-colored vans.

A few minutes later, Violet stomped in, her eyes red-rimmed. "*What*?" she demanded.

I held up my hands, like *whoa.* "Nothing. I didn't say anything."

"You were staring at me."

"I was not." I leaned back in my chair. "I just looked up because I heard you come in. Sheesh. Excuse me for breathing."

She snorted. "Right. Mr. Perfect. Look at you, taking care of the little ones. Always kissing up, aren't you?"

My face felt warm. "I'm not kissing up," I said. "It just looks like that because *you* never help with anything." It was true—Violet just did what she wanted. She was pretty much the most selfish person I'd ever met. And someone had to look after the twins. Not that Mom didn't—she adored them—but a lot of the time she had other things she needed to do. I'd always helped take care of them, ever since they were babies.

"Whatever," Violet said, dismissing me. "So, what, you're playing school?"

"We're *designing*," Saffron said. "For painting the van."

Violet moved closer and studied the papers spread across the table. "Seriously? Don't tell me this is the plan."

"Do you like it?" Saffron asked eagerly.

"Sure. It's all just freaking fabulous, Saffy. Bee costumes and a striped Ford van."

"What's wrong with Fords?" Saffron asked, putting down her yellow marker.

"Nothing," I told her.

"You know what Ford stands for?" Violet said.

Saffron shook her head.

Violet gave her an evil smile. "Found On Road Dead." Then she spelled it out slowly, as if we were all idiots: "*F-O-R-D.* Get it?"

Whisper's eyes widened.

"Or Fix Often, Repair Daily."

"Not *our* van," Saffron said. "Dad's already fixed it all up. We're going to call it George."

"We are?" This was the first I'd heard of it.

"Yes."

"Ford Owners R Dumb," Violet said. "Fast Only Rolling Downhill."

"Okay, Vile. Enough already."

"Don't call me that." Violet raised a hand like she was going to hit me, then slowly lowered it and turned back to Saffron, smiling meanly.

"You know what *Ford* spelled backward stands for?" she asked.

Saffron shrugged. "I don't care."

"Driver Returns on Foot."

Saffron put her hands on her hips and gave Violet the evil eye right back. "And Whisper and Wolf don't care either."

Violet rolled her eyes. "What*ever*."

"And George doesn't care EITHER!" And with that, Saffron turned away from Violet and back to her drawing.

So there, Vile, I thought.

Three

WHISPER ISN'T MY sister's real name. Her birth certificate says Juniper Sage Brooks. We've never called her Juniper though. When she was a baby we called her Bean, because she was so tiny.

She and Saffy aren't identical twins: Saffron's always been way bigger, right from when they were born. Plus Saffy has red hair and pale skin with tons of freckles, like Mom and me. Mom's family was from Scotland, a couple of generations back, and my friend Duncan says Scotland has more redheads than anywhere else. Curtis's dad was from Guyana—he was part black and part Indian and part white, Curtis says. So Curtis and Violet and Whisper all have light brown skin and dark eyes and super-long eyelashes. They're all skinny and athletic-looking too. None of them actually does any sports, but they're naturally good at that kind of thing, just like I'm naturally terrible. Curtis calls Violet and Whisper his *mini-me's*, even though they're girls, which I think is dumb. *Mini-me's*. It'd be dumb even if they were boys.

We all left Lasqueti Island and moved to Victoria when I was nine. By that time, Saffron was talking up a storm and Whisper wasn't saying much at all, and when she did, it was in a tiny whisper so you had to bend your head close to hear her. Mom used to get mad at people for comparing the two of them. She said it wasn't fair, especially since Saffron was such a chatterbox.

It was around that time that we started calling her Whisper instead of Bean. Then she and Saffy started going to preschool, and their teacher was worried because Whisper wouldn't talk. She still whispered to us at home, but she wouldn't say a word to the teachers or the other kids. Mom said that preschool was unnatural anyway. She said little kids belonged at home with their families and pulled the twins out of the program.

But now Whisper was five and in kindergarten, and she still didn't speak to anyone outside our family. She'd been going to school all year and hadn't said one word there, except maybe to Saffron if no one else was around. Curtis tried to push her to talk sometimes, to say hi to the neighbors or whatever, but she never would. She'd just stare down at the ground or hide behind her dad's legs. Mom said she'd talk when she was ready, and that this trip would be good for her.

I wasn't so sure. Whisper didn't like change. She only ate six things—macaroni, Ritz crackers, apples, bread with peanut butter, bananas and orange cheddar cheese. Plus chocolate, which didn't count because Mom wouldn't buy it. Whisper hated loud noises, like car horns and people shouting. She had wicked meltdowns. A lot of them. And not to be mean, but I wasn't sure I wanted to share a tent with someone who still wet the bed on a regular basis.

That weekend we painted the van—all of us except Violet, who had taken off somewhere with Ty, saying that if she was going to have to be away for God knew how long, she should at least be able to spend the weekend with him.

On Saturday Mom and I took the sketches the twins had made and used them to come up with a design, while Curtis sanded old paint and rust off the van. The design part was easy—solid black on the front and back, yellow stripes on a black background for the sides—but the sanding took forever. Mom and I helped. We put on dust masks and scoured and polished until our arms and shoulders ached.

It was warm for May, the sun high in the sky, and Curtis had stripped off his T-shirt. I could see the ropy muscles in his back and shoulders shifting under his skin. I wished I had muscles like that. You couldn't see my muscles at all. Sometimes I took my shirt off and looked in the bathroom mirror, hoping to see something other than pale, freckly pudginess, but things in that department seemed to be getting worse rather than better.

"You're burning," Mom said, touching the back of my neck lightly. "You should put on some coconut oil."

She didn't like sunscreen, because of all the chemicals in it, but I wasn't crazy about smelling like a coconut. "It doesn't work," I said. "I burn anyway."

"Go get a shirt with a collar then."

"Fine," I said. I was glad of an excuse to take a break. I headed into the house and poured myself a glass of cold water.

"Is it time to paint George?" Saffron called from the living room. "Whisper wants to know."

"No," I said. "Maybe this evening."

"Want to watch this with us?"

I drained my glass, left it in the sink and wandered into the living room, where the twins were curled up on the couch. "Whatcha watching?"

"*Ice Age Three*."

I watched the screen for a minute. They had the volume turned down so low I could barely hear it. "Want me to turn that up for you?"

Whisper shook her head.

"We know all the words anyway," Saffron told me.

I probably did too. They must have seen it a hundred times, since it was the only DVD they owned that wasn't an educational nature documentary. Mom wasn't a fan of television, but she wasn't a fan of rules either, so the twins mostly did whatever they wanted.

"I should get back to work," I said. I grabbed a long-sleeved shirt from a pile of clean laundry, slipped it on over my T-shirt and was about to head back outside when I heard the phone ring close by. The twins didn't lift their eyes from the screen.

I looked around, following the sound, and finally found the phone under a pile of blankets on the couch. "Move your butt, Whisper," I said, grabbing it. "Hello?"

"Hello. Is that Jade?"

I tried to lower my voice. "No. It's Wolf."

"Oh, sorry, Wolf. You sound so much like your mom."

"Uh-huh." I hate when people say that.

"It's Susan."

Violet's mom. "Hi," I said. "Did you want to talk to Violet? She's not here right now."

"I know," she said. "She showed up here."

"She did?" I tried to hide my surprise. Susan lives a good forty-minute drive away, in Sooke. More important, Violet and Susan do not get along. I mean, Violet doesn't exactly get along with anyone, but she *really* doesn't get along with her mom.

"With a boy."

"Oh. Ty."

"Apparently. She says you're all going off on some crazy trip."

"Just for the summer," I said. "A family holiday." That's what Mom told me to say if people at school got too nosy. Susan wasn't a teacher, but she was closer to that category than the family category. I'd only met her a few times. She seemed a lot older than my mom, and she wore a lot of makeup and had long painted fingernails that Mom said were fake. I was pretty sure she wouldn't understand our plans.

"It's hardly a secret," she said. "I've just read your mother's website. Every wacky word."

"Oh," I said, feeling stupid. I could picture Susan's narrow face, her small mouth pursed in annoyance. "Right."

"Can I talk to Jade, please?"

Susan and Curtis couldn't talk without fighting, so it was always my mom Susan talked to about Violet-related stuff. "I'll get her," I said. Then I covered the phone with one hand and yelled, "Mom!"

"Come out here if you want to talk to me!" she shouted back.

"Phone!"

She came in, dust mask dangling around her neck and a rusty line running across her cheeks and over her nose. "Who is it?"

"Susan." I handed her the phone.

She wrinkled her nose, wiped her hands on her jeans and took the phone from me. "Susan?" A long pause. I could hear the angry buzz of Susan's voice but couldn't make out what she was saying. "Uh-huh. Well, that's up to you...No, of course Curtis and I want her to come with us..."

Mom dropped to the couch beside the twins, holding the phone a couple of inches from her ear. "I know she doesn't want to..." *Buzz.* "Well, I think not wanting to leave her boyfriend is a big part of it...She does? Did she say that to you?" *Buzz buzz buzz.* "Let me talk to her." *Buzz.* "I don't care if she doesn't want to."

At that point Mom noticed me listening and shooed me away. I didn't move. She put her hand over the phone. "Wolf. Go help Curtis."

I headed back outside, sat down on a wooden block near the van and watched Curtis. He was using a finer grit sandpaper now, polishing the surface smooth. "That was Susan," I told him. "On the phone."

He grunted. "What's she want?"

"Violet's over there."

He stopped sanding and turned to look at me. "She is?"

"Uh-huh. With Ty."

"What's that about?"

I shrugged. "I dunno. She really doesn't want to go on this trip."

"Yeah?"

"Susan called it a crazy trip. And she called Mom wacky."

"Crazy? She said that?"

I nodded. Waited. I could see a muscle twitching in his jaw.

"What's *crazy* is staying here," he said. "What's *crazy* is sticking to this whole system of jobs and buying stuff and worrying about what people think." His voice was getting louder. "What's *crazy* is buying a new house and paying someone to lay down turf for a lawn, like Susan just did. A bloody lawn! The bees are dying, the world economy is on the edge of total collapse, and she's thinking about her lawn. That's what's *crazy*."

"I know," I said. "I know."

He snorted and pulled his dust mask back down over his nose and mouth. "You can't eat a lawn," he said, turning his attention back to the van. "Someone oughtta tell her that."

I picked up a new sheet of sandpaper and watched Mom walk out of the house and toward us. Her hair was in a long braid to keep it out of the way, and she was twisting it between her fingers.

"Wolf tells me Susan's got her panties in a knot," Curtis said, looking up at her without pausing in his sanding. *Scritch scritch, scritch scritch.*

Mom sighed. "Violet's upset about missing school and leaving Ty. She asked Susan if she could stay with her for the summer."

"Violet's not thinking straight." He shook his head. "Susan would have her in summer camps and piano lessons. She'd have her in bed by nine. Vi would have about as much chance of seeing Ty as she would if she was halfway across the country with us."

"It's a moot point anyway," Mom said. "Susan said no. She doesn't want her."

"Yeah," Curtis said.

They were both quiet for a minute. I couldn't imagine my mom ever, ever, *ever* turning me or the twins away. Couldn't imagine her not wanting us around. Even if I'd just been at school for the day, when I came in the door she always gave me a big hug and said she'd missed me.

For a moment, I even felt a tiny bit sorry for Violet.

On Sunday, we painted the van. It didn't turn out quite like I'd imagined. The black was kind of patchy and uneven—I guess maybe we should have sanded more or used a glossier paint—and the stripes were more neon-lime than honeybee-yellow. Still, it was done, and the twins seemed happy enough about it.

And then we started packing. Even though Curtis had said there was lots of storage, the van filled up fast. There was the tool box, the tent, sleeping bags, dishes and cooking stuff, cans of food, boxes of pasta, toilet paper, Whisper's night-time diapers, jugs of water…It all disappeared into the space beneath the mattress. Mom said Violet and I could pack a small bag each. I packed a pair of jeans, a pair of shorts, underwear and a couple of T-shirts, a hoodie and my tooth-brush. I managed to cram in my ancient iPod and a couple of graphic novels, plus a few pens and a blank notebook in case I had time to do any drawing.

Mom and Curtis were packing up the rest of the house. Most of the furniture wasn't ours anyway, since we'd rented the place furnished. Stuff we wanted to keep—like our photos and clothes and books and the twins' toys—we packed into boxes for Curtis to put in our new storage locker. We'd rented it for a whole year with the money we would've used for June's rent. Which was pretty awesome, when you thought about it. If we were ever really broke, we could just live in that storage locker, no problem.

I wandered through the house, looking at each room, silently saying goodbye. We'd only lived here for three years, but it felt like home. It was weird to be leaving. I wondered if we'd ever live somewhere again, or if we'd just drive from place to place forever. Mom wouldn't talk about what we'd do once we arrived on the east coast. *We'll take it as it comes,* she'd said. *One day at a time. We'll be free, Wolf. Not tied down to any place. We can follow our hearts.*

You could tell it made her happy, the idea of all that freedom. Not me. I *liked* being tied down to a place. I liked our house, the park behind us, the potholed tarmac of our dead-end road. I liked the huge Garry oak trees and the deer that ate our cedar hedge. I liked my friends. I got a lump in my throat imagining going to school in the morning and telling everyone that it was my last day. My teacher Katie, my friend Duncan…even Ginger, the fat grumpy school cat who spent his days curled up on the wide window ledge in the main classroom. Even *Caitlin*, who made a point of saying at least one mean thing to me every day.

I sat down on my bedroom floor, unpacked my notebook, tore out a blank sheet of paper and wrote down my email address over and over. In the morning, I'd give it to everyone at school. Mom was bringing her laptop on the trip because she had to keep the blog updated and post videos to YouTube and stuff. I didn't know how often we'd have Wi-Fi, but hopefully I'd be able to stay in touch.

From downstairs, I heard the sound of the front door opening and then slamming closed. Then I heard Curtis, loud and angry: "So you decided to show up after all, did you? Decided you didn't want to get left behind?"

Violet was home. I'd been kind of hoping we'd have to leave without her.

Four

THE NEXT MORNING I told my friend Duncan about the change in plans. "So you know how we're doing this trip? This summer?"

Duncan didn't take his eyes off his computer screen. "Yeah. The save-the-bees thing."

I logged into the computer beside his. "We're going to leave sooner than I thought."

"Uh-huh."

I moved the mouse in circles and watched the cursor dance around the desktop icons. "So, this is my last day, probably," I said.

Duncan swiveled his chair toward me and studied me through the gaps in his curtain of dark tangled hair. I used to have long hair too, until last year when I got tired of people thinking I was a girl. Violet cut it for me and made a real mess, so it ended up way too short. I never knew how much my ears stuck out until I had no hair to hide them. It's grown back somewhat. Enough to cover my ears anyway.

"Seriously, dude?" Duncan said at last. "You're not messing with me?"

"Yeah. I mean, no, I'm not messing—"

"You're gonna get to miss the rest of school?"

I shrugged. "My mom says I can homeschool."

"Huh. So, like, she'd be your teacher? That kinda sucks." He turned back to his computer and typed furiously for a few minutes, then looked up at me and spoke again. "I've been working on a new game. Want to see?"

"Sure." I rolled my chair closer to his so that I could see his screen. It showed a green and purple landscape with a cartoony helicopter hovering overhead. "Cool. What do you do?"

"Not much yet. You control the helicopter with the arrow keys. Space bar to shoot."

"Shoot what?"

Duncan clicked open a menu, scrolled down a list and typed something in. "Don't know yet. I still have to add the bad guys. Enemies. Bosses. You know how some games have those health bars? To show how many shots left for a kill?"

I nodded.

"I'm gonna do that."

"Cool." Ginger butted his head against my ankles, purring, and I picked him up. He weighed a ton, and his fur was all matted around his neck and under his ears. "Ginger has dreadlocks," I said. "Little cat dreads." I tried to tease one of the tangles apart, but the cat stiffened, gave a squawky meow and jumped down.

Across the room, our teacher, Katie, looked up. She was sitting on the floor with a group of kids who were building a sculpture from tin cans and recycled electronics. "All good?" she called.

"Dude just told me today's his last day," Duncan said.

Katie stood up, brushed off her jeans and walked over to us. "Really, Wolf? You're leaving?"

"My mom didn't tell you?"

"No." She put her hand on my shoulder. "So what's going on?"

I liked Katie too much to give her the family-vacation line. "Uh, have you ever looked at my mom's website?"

"I didn't even know she had one."

I typed in the address and beckoned to Katie to come around to my side of the computer so she could see the screen. "There," I said. "Read that. Starting at *My name is Jade Everett.*"

Katie leaned toward the screen. Her dark pink hair hung around her face like the feathers of some tropical bird, and I could see her eyes scanning back and forth behind her black-framed glasses as she read. My hands were sweaty, and I wiped them on my jeans. I was doing exactly what Mom had told me not to do.

"Wolf, have you read this?" Katie turned to me.

I nodded. "Yeah. Of course."

Katie's pale cheeks were flushed. "When…she says here that she doesn't expect to see her kids reach adulthood… I'm sure she doesn't mean that literally, you know? That it's just…that she's…"

"Going for maximum impact," Duncan put in helpfully. "Exaggeration. Hyperbole."

Katie snapped her fingers. "Right. *Hyperbole*. Nice word, Duncan."

I didn't say anything. I was pretty sure my mom meant it literally.

"Wolf? Are you okay?"

"Yeah, fine."

"I mean…" Katie touched her fingers to her lips. Her cheeks were still very pink, almost the same color as her hair. "I mean, you're not, you know, worried that the world is about to end?"

I shook my head. "No. Well, not *too* worried. I mean, we all know there are some pretty big problems, right?"

"Sure. I mean, I think it's great your family is doing this. I just wanted to make sure you're not, uh…"

"Freaking out," Duncan supplied.

Katie looked at me.

"Really," I said. "I'm fine."

"And your sisters? The twins? They're going too?"

"Of course. What else would they do?"

Katie waved a hand at the computer screen. "Do they know about all this?"

"They can't read," I said. "But Mom's told them we have to help people understand about the bees. How important they are, stuff like that."

She relaxed slightly. "Just that Juniper seems like such an anxious little girl. I wouldn't want her to be worrying about adult problems."

If the bees all died, it wasn't just going to be adults who had problems. "Nah, she's all right," I said. "She and Saffron are excited about the trip."

"Good." Katie squeezed my shoulder. "I hope you'll keep in touch. Let us know how it's going."

"I will," I said. And all of a sudden there was this lump in my throat and a stinging in my eyes, and I had to look away so that she and Duncan wouldn't see me not-quite-crying.

Duncan and I took our lunches outside and sat on a wooden bench. It was sunny and almost warm down here, with the buildings blocking the breeze. I unzipped my hoodie and opened my lunch box. I'd brought leftover chili, but I didn't feel hungry.

"Can't believe you're leaving," Duncan said.

"Yeah. It's weird."

"You'll be back though. Right? I mean, in September?"

"Yeah, maybe."

"Maybe? Like, ninety percent chance? Fifty percent chance? What are we talking here?"

I shrugged. "Mom says she doesn't want to plan ahead, you know? Just, like, take it as it comes and see what happens."

Duncan didn't say anything for a minute. We watched the little kids—Saffron and Whisper and half a dozen others were playing some kind of tag, dashing this way and that, the game punctuated by loud squeals and protests. *That's not fair!*

The rule is, you have to count to five. No, ten. No, we changed it to five. Saffron was the loudest and the bossiest—she could hold her own with the second- and third-graders—and Whisper, as always, was her silent shadow.

Finally, Duncan gave a long sigh. "Dude, no offense, but that blog of your mom's? That's some pretty crazy stuff."

"Yeah."

"You know. Intense. I read it and I was, like, what the photon?"

"Uh-huh."

"You believe all that? Like, that the world is, you know." He made air quotes with his fingers. "*These last doomed years.* All that stuff?"

I shrugged. "I guess so, yeah. I mean, not like this week or anything, but…"

"Huh."

"I mean, maybe not, right? If people get together and change the way we treat the planet." I looked at the side of the shed behind the vegetable garden, where the kids from a few years back had painted a giant mural of Earth—a slightly lopsided, blue-and-green planet Earth with little people standing around its edges. "That's why we're doing this trip."

"So you want to do it? You're into it?"

I shook my head. "Not really. But…well, I guess it's important, right? So. Yeah. You know."

"Yeah." Duncan peeled the lid off a yogurt container and fumbled around in his lunch bag. "Dude, do you have a spoon? My mom forgot to put one in here."

I shook my head.

"Wolf?" Katie was standing behind us in the doorway. "Your mother's here."

"She is?"

"To pick you up. Can you tell your sisters to get their jackets and bags?"

I nodded and she disappeared back into the school.

"So," Duncan said. "I guess I'll see you around."

"Yeah. See you." I felt like I should say something more, but I couldn't think of anything, so I just walked over to where the little kids were playing. "Saffy! Whisper!"

They both stopped running and looked up at me. Saffron put her hands on her hips, ready to argue with whatever I was about to say. "What?"

"Mom's here. We gotta go. Get your coats and the rest of your things, okay?"

"Now?"

"Yeah, now." I started back toward the school and they followed me. "I'll meet you in the front hall, okay?"

Saffron nodded, took Whisper's hand, and they headed down the stairs to the basement. I went the other way, to my classroom, and grabbed my jacket. I had a ton of stuff in my cubby—a whole year's worth of projects, half-written stories, artwork—and I started to gather it up. Then I stopped. What was I going to do with it? There was no way I could bring it in the van, and we had already packed up the house. I was still standing there with all these papers in my arms when I heard my mom's voice coming from the little office by the front door.

"I'd think that you, of all people, would understand," she was saying.

I could hear Katie's quieter voice replying, and I strained to make out the words. "I do, I do. It's just…" And then some murmuring that I couldn't quite catch.

"Seems a bit hypocritical," Mom said. "I guess all the talk about the environment and sustainability, etcetera etcetera, is just that: talk."

"That's not fair," Katie said. She sounded angry, and her voice was louder now. "And it's not true. We're—"

Mom cut her off. "Look, I know you think you're contributing. And I know that this place makes more effort than most schools. But honestly, do you really think that recycling and composting and riding bikes on field trips is going to save the planet?"

"We all do what we can."

"Well, it isn't enough. You have to think about the big picture here—"

"Jade—"

Mom cut her off again. "You think showing kids a few videos on global warming is going to lead to a generation of activists? You think we have that kind of time? These kids can't grow up to save the world if there's nothing left for them to save."

"Jade. Listen. This is what I'm worried about—this world-is-about-to-end thing. How do you think hearing that is going to affect your kids?"

"I don't think hearing it will hurt them nearly as much as letting it happen! I don't think it will hurt them as much as seeing the people they love starving and dying." Mom's words hung in the still air. My heart was fluttering, all light and irregular-feeling, like an injured bird flapping about in my rib cage.

"Shhh, shhh," Katie said. She lowered her voice so I couldn't make out her words. I stepped closer, quietly moving toward the half-closed office door and straining to hear.

"Wolf?" Saffron's voice.

I turned. Saffron and Whisper were standing there, hoodies and backpacks in their arms. I wondered how much they had heard. "Hey, you two," I said loudly. "Ready to roll?"

Mom stepped out of the office, her face flushed. "Okay, kids. Let's go."

Behind her, Katie waved to us. "Have a good summer," she said, like she hadn't just had a huge argument with our mother. "Take care of yourselves."

Saffron darted forward and gave her a hug. I stared at the floor.

Outside, a horn honked loudly.

"Come on," Mom said. "Curtis and Violet are waiting in the van."

I followed her down the steps, holding Whisper's hand in mine. Saffron skipped ahead, flapping her arms as if she already had her bee costume on. As I got into the van, I glanced back at the school. Katie was watching us from the window, holding a squirming Ginger in her arms. I waved goodbye as we drove off, but she didn't wave back. She probably couldn't even see me through the van's tinted windows.

Five

IT TOOK FORTY minutes to drive to the Swartz Bay ferry terminal, and Violet argued with Curtis for every single one of them. I put on my headphones, closed my eyes and listened to music on my iPod. Saffy went to sleep—she always slept on long drives—and Whisper played a game on Violet's phone.

Even with my headphones on, I could hear Violet's heated voice. I cranked the volume until it drowned her out and I could only see her mouth moving and the angry tears tracing lines of mascara down her cheeks. She was always so dramatic. It wasn't like I wanted to be going away, but it was happening anyway and there was no point fighting it. When something is inevitable, you might as well quit struggling and make the best of the situation.

Violet never seemed to get that.

We arrived at the ferry terminal just in time to see the one
o'clock ferry pulling away, which meant we had to wait two
hours for the next one. Mom and Curtis went inside to the
coffee shop, Vi sat in the car, sulking, and I took the twins to
the playground area and watched them swing on the monkey
bars. Whisper made it all the way across easily, kicking her
skinny legs and grinning with delight. Saffy was heavier and
less agile but fiercely determined. The tip of her tongue stuck
out in concentration as she battled her way across, grunting
with the effort.

The weekend's warm weather had been chased away by
thick gray clouds, and a cold wind was blowing off the water.
I buried my hands in my jacket pockets and found the little
pieces of paper with my email address on them. I'd forgotten
to give them to everyone at school.

As soon as we were all back in the van and driving onto the
ferry, Violet resumed her argument, picking right up where
she'd left off.

"You're doing this just to get me away from Ty, aren't
you? That's what this trip is about. You want us to break up."

Curtis looked at her in the rearview mirror. "That is
not what this trip is about, and you know it." He sounded
angry, and I didn't blame him. Violet had to be the most

self-centered person in the world if she really thought this was all about her.

"It's not about you and Ty," Saffy said. She patted Violet's denim-clad thigh. "It's so that we can stop everyone starving and dying. Right, Mom?"

Instinctively, I turned to look at Whisper, who was sitting behind us in the single bucket seat. Her eyes were enormous dark pools.

"That's not going to happen," Curtis said. He pointed out the window. "See that, Saffy? We're driving right onto the ferry! Look, it's like a parking lot on a boat!"

Saffron was not that easily distracted. "I heard Mom say it. At my school."

"That's not what I said," Mom protested.

"It is SO!"

"Saffron, chill. It's not going to happen, because people like us aren't going to let it," Curtis said.

Violet snorted. "Yeah, right. Like we're so powerful."

I dug my elbow into her side, hard.

"Ow! Dad, Wolf hit me."

"I did not." I peeked at Whisper again. She still looked wide-eyed and scared. I tried to think of a way to change the subject. "Ty's probably relieved you're going away," I told Violet. "You're always complaining about something."

"And you're always being a total loser," she snapped. "A stupid *fat* loser."

"Enough." Curtis inched close to the car in front of us and slammed the van into *park* with a jolt. "Both of you, just shut up."

Mom shook her head. "Everyone's overtired," she said. "Wolf, how about you take the twins upstairs to the play area? Curtis and I have work to do." She picked up the laptop bag. "I need to update the website, and I thought I'd tweet a photo of us setting out."

"Great idea," Curtis said. "Everyone line up and say 'cheese.'"

We all clambered out—Violet managing to stomp on my foot in the process—and stood in a row with our backs to the bee-striped van. Curtis tried to find somewhere to stand where he could fit us all into the frame, which wasn't easy among the jam-packed cars on the ferry's vehicle deck. "Okay, kids—smile!"

I smiled. Saffron and Whisper smiled. Violet stuck out her tongue. Mom, who was standing with her arms around the twins, glared at her. "Can we please just get this done?" she said. Her voice was tight, like she was talking with her jaw clenched shut.

"*You* can do what you like," Violet said. "Leave me out of it." And she flounced off, pushing through a cluster of other passengers and through the doorway that led to the stairs to the upper decks.

Mom started after her, but Curtis called out, "Let her go, Jade. She needs some time to cool off."

"Fine," Mom said. She hoisted the strap of the laptop bag onto her shoulder. "God, I hope the whole trip isn't going to be like this."

So did I.

℮

Most people who live on Vancouver Island probably take the ferry to the mainland all the time. Not me though. I'd only been on it once, two years earlier, to spend a weekend with some old friends of Mom and Curtis—people they knew from their Lasqueti Island days. We'd gone to the science center, which had been really cool, and to some market-type place, where we'd eaten little hot donuts out of a paper bag.

"Do you remember when we took this boat before?" I asked the twins as we headed up the stairs.

"I never did," Saffron said, and Whisper shook her head.

"You were only three," I told them. "Really little."

Saffron looked skeptical, so I dropped it. "Want to go to the play area?"

"I guess," Saffron said. "This doesn't seem like a boat."

I laughed. "I know. It's huge. It even has shops and restaurants."

"Really?" She did a little hop-skip-jump. "Can we see them?"

"Sure." I grinned at her. "We can see everything. You want to see everything too, Whisper?"

Whisper's smile stretched all the way across her face.

Sometimes when I was with the twins, I felt like I could see things through their eyes, just for a little bit. Mostly, it meant everything looked bigger and better and more exciting. Once in a while though—like in the van when Saffron repeated Mom's words about people starving to death and stuff—it meant everything looked bigger and scarier. I didn't think Mom should let the twins hear that kind of talk. Maybe it was disloyal of me, but I thought Katie was right about that.

The three of us trooped through the restaurant and the coffee bar, the gift shop, the tiny video arcade, and checked out the kids' play area—which Saffron dismissed as *for babies*—before heading outside. The wind was ferocious, and we ran along the slippery metal deck, facing into the wild gusty air and feeling it pushing back against us.

I looked down over the railing at the water five decks below. It was a dark, indescribable color—a mix of gray, green and blue—and you could see the swirls made by the strong currents. We were going between two islands, and the dark water and the gray rocks and the green trees reminded me of when we lived on Lasqueti.

"I'm a kite!" Saffron shrieked, her jacket unzipped and her arms held out like wings. "The wind's going to pick me up!"

I laughed, watching her, but then I heard a frightened sob behind me. I turned and saw Whisper huddled in a little ball against one of the massive life-raft chests. "Whisper? Hey, what is it?"

Saffron stopped running. "You don't like the wind?"

Whisper's wails got louder, her shoulders shaking. I picked her up—she was such a lightweight, just skin and bone and stringy little muscles. "Come on, it's okay—we'll go inside."

She shook her head violently and put her hands over her ears.

"Whisper, what is it?" I asked. "What's wrong?" She was squirming and kicking and howling in my ear, and I had to put her down. Her face was beet red and streaked with tears. "What is it?" I was pleading with her, desperate to make her stop. "What do you *want*?"

Saffron patted her shoulder. "Don't be scared."

I wondered if it was the wind or if it was more than that. What Mom had said at the school—it wasn't like she hadn't said that kind of thing before, but she wasn't usually so blunt about it around the twins. Maybe it had really freaked Whisper out. Then again, Whisper often had meltdowns. I looked at her, feeling helpless. "Come on, kiddo. Can you tell me what's wrong?"

She shook her head.

"She doesn't talk anymore," Saffron said matter-of-factly. "Not even to me."

I stared at her, trying to think when I had last heard Whisper speak. On Saturday, for sure—she'd said she wanted to paint the van like a bee. That had been two days ago. "Whisper, you can tell us what's wrong. Okay? Just whisper it." I bent my head close.

Nothing.

"Saffy, you ask her."

Saffron shrugged. "What's wrong, Whisper? Are you scared?" She asked it in a funny baby voice, like she was playing a game with her dolls or something.

Whisper didn't speak.

It was starting to rain, the drops icy cold and wind driven. I ducked my head. "I'm going to pick you up again, okay? We'll go inside." This time, when I picked her up, she didn't fight me. She went limp in my arms and put her head down on my shoulder. Saffron ran ahead and struggled to open the heavy door against the wind, and we all slipped inside. I shifted Whisper's weight in my arms, and as my hand gripped her skinny thigh, I realized that she was wet.

As in, not from the rain.

I decided not to mention it. I stuck my hand in my jacket pocket and jingled my loose change. I still had twelve dollars left from my birthday money.

"Do you guys want to get a treat?" Mom wouldn't like it—she had healthy snacks for us in the car—but there was still almost an hour to go, and I didn't think I could handle another meltdown.

Whisper nodded her head against my shoulder. I put her down and we walked in the direction of the coffee bar. The sleeve of my hoodie was wet from her pants. I rubbed it against the dry fabric of the ferry seats as we walked past the rows, trying to dry it off.

Violet already thought I was a stupid fat loser. All I needed was a jacket that smelled like pee.

Six

I BOUGHT THE twins a pack of Smarties to share—sugar *and* coloring; Mom would flip if she found out—and got myself a hot chocolate and a bag of Doritos. Someone had left a copy of the *Vancouver Sun* on the table, and the headlines were all about wars and people being killed in other countries. I folded it over so the twins wouldn't see the pictures. My brain felt all twitchy, like it was hopping from one worry to another.

"Yo."

I turned as a hand landed on my shoulder. *Ty.* And beside him, clutching his arm like it was a life ring, Violet.

"What are you doing here?" I blurted. I looked at Violet. "Mom said he couldn't come."

Ty shrugged. "Your mom doesn't own the ferry, little man."

"I know that." Ty had this way of making me feel stupid. He was seventeen, which was practically an adult, and he had piercings—not just in his ears, but in his bottom lip and one eyebrow and even his tongue. Violet thought this was cool—she wanted to get one in her nose—but I didn't understand why anyone would want holes in their face.

Violet smirked at me. "She doesn't own the highway either."

"Duh," I said. Violet was only three years older than I was, but she acted like the difference was way more than that. She stared at me, all smug-faced, and I realized I had no idea what she was talking about. "Uh, what do you mean?" I asked. "About the highway?"

"I *mean*," she said, "that Jade thinks she can break us up. But she can't."

"This trip's not all about you," I said. Then I regretted it, because what it was about—the bees vanishing and all that stuff—wasn't something I wanted the twins thinking about. I stood up, stepped away from the table and beckoned to Violet to come closer.

"What?" She looked annoyed, but she let go of Ty's arm and followed me. "What is it?"

I lowered my voice. "Saffy says Whisper doesn't talk anymore. At all."

"Sure she does."

"Are you sure? Because I can't remember her saying anything for a couple of days."

"So ask her something."

"Like what?"

Violet rolled her eyes. "It doesn't matter, doofus. Just see if she answers."

"You ask her." I thought back to Whisper's meltdown on the ferry deck, and my stomach twisted. Sometimes I felt like some little creature was alive in there, squirming around, poking at me from inside, demanding…I didn't know what. Definitely demanding something though. I wrapped my arms around my middle and squeezed.

Violet walked back over to the table. "Hey, Whisper, can I have a Smartie?"

Whisper nodded and pushed the pack toward her.

Violet gave me a sideways look. I raised my eyebrows, like *see*?

"Can I have red? Or do you like those best?"

Whisper slid a red Smartie toward Violet's outstretched hand.

"Thanks, kiddo." Violet popped it into her mouth. "So, you two ready for tomorrow?"

"What's tomorrow?" Saffy asked.

"Our first opportunity to make big fools of ourselves in public."

I shook my head at her. "Violet. Don't." The creature in my stomach gave another twist, and I crammed a handful of Doritos into my mouth to pacify it.

"What do you mean?" Saffy asked.

"Uh, downtown? At the art gallery? Right out front somewhere, like on the steps or something?" Violet looked at Ty, who she was totally showing off for. "Jade's first presentation?"

"It's not exactly a presentation," I said. "It's, like, guerrilla theater."

Ty laughed. "Gorillas? I thought you were gonna be bees."

46

Saffron frowned, her lower lip sticking out. "I *am* going to be a bee."

Ty made an *ooo-ooo* monkey noise and pretended to scratch his armpit.

"Shut up, Ty," I said. "Guerrilla, like *G-U-E*. Not gorilla like the monkey. Guerrilla theater's, like, performance art. But, you know, political."

"He knows," Violet said. "I've told him."

Ty was still making monkey noises. Whisper was looking down at the table, sliding her Smarties into same-color groups: red, pink, orange, yellow, green, purple, blue, brown. I've always wondered why they make brown Smarties when no one really likes them. Duncan told me once that there used to be two shades of brown. He always knows weird things like that because he reads Wikipedia all the time.

"Ty! Stop it," Saffron ordered. "You look stupid."

Ty stopped *ooo-ooo*ing and turned to Vi. "You told me about this guerilla thing?"

"Yeah. Don't you remember?" Violet stole a Dorito from my bag and crunched it loudly. "Like some of the protests back during the Vietnam war. Or in the nineties, when people were trying to get the government to do more to fight AIDS? They pretended they were dying right there on the streets. They even carried coffins and stuff."

We'd watched a documentary about it with Mom. Some of the stuff the protesters had done was pretty awesome. And it had worked too—they'd made people pay attention.

"What do bees have to do with AIDS?" Ty asked.

I rolled my eyes. "Nothing, Ty. That was just an example."

Violet glared at me. "It can be about anything, Ty. It's, like, a way to make people listen."

"There's this group, Circus something," I said. "Mom spent a couple years in New York before I was born, and she did some stuff with them. Theater stuff, about poverty and gay rights. But then she got more into the environment." I shrugged. "And, you know, bees."

"Right. Bees." Ty grinned at me. "I guess I'll see you all in action tomorrow then." He lifted his arms like he was flying. "Buzz, buzz, buzz."

I poured the last of the Dorito crumbs into the palm of my hand and stuffed them into my mouth. Mom had made bee costumes for me and the twins, and she was expecting us to wear them. Violet had gotten out of it, partly because she was older and partly because Jade wasn't really her mom, but mostly because she was better at saying no than I was.

"Let's go," Violet said, tugging on Ty's arm. She looked at me. "You've got orange cheese crud all over your face."

I wiped my mouth with my sleeve and watched them walk away. Then I sat back down at the table with the twins, folded my arms on the newspaper and laid my head on them.

I didn't want to be here.

"What's wrong, Wolf?" Saffron asked.

"Nothing."

"You look sad."

I straightened up. "I'm okay." I tried to smile at her. "Are you excited about our trip, Saffy?"

"I guess so," she said.

Whisper had put her fingertip on top of a green Smartie and was driving it around the table like it was a car. "How about you?" I asked her. "Are you excited?"

She nodded, but she didn't look up at me.

I bent my head, trying to catch her eye. "Hey. Are you worried about something? You can talk to me, you know."

Saffron gave a loud, dramatic sigh. "I *told* you. She *can't* talk."

Seven

AN ANNOUNCEMENT CAME over the loudspeakers—
"We are nearing the Tsawwassen terminal. It is now time for
all passengers to return to the vehicle decks"—and the twins
and I trudged back down the stairs. I couldn't remember
exactly where we had parked, but our bee-striped van wasn't
too hard to find. Mom and Curtis were already there, sitting
in the front seats, studying a map.

"Where's Violet?" Mom asked.

I shrugged and helped Whisper buckle up her seat belt.
I wasn't going to be the one to bring up the subject of Ty.

Saffron was less cautious. "She's with her boyfriend," she
announced.

Mom twisted around to face us. "What?"

"Ty's on the ferry," I said, slipping back into my own seat.
"We saw them up in the coffee shop."

Mom turned and looked at Curtis. "You deal with this.
I'm so done with her right now."

Curtis drummed his fingers on the steering wheel. "Maybe she just ran into him. Maybe he's going to Vancouver for some other reason."

Mom didn't say anything.

"Where are we staying tonight?" I asked. "I mean, are we camping? Or…"

"In Vancouver? No. We'll stay with Eva and Mary." She put her hand on Curtis's arm. "I should call and let them know we're on our way. They were probably expecting us to be on the earlier ferry."

"Who's Eva and Mary?" Saffron asked.

"Who *are*. Not who is," I corrected her.

"Old friends of mine," Mom said. "You remember them, Wolf?"

"Um…"

"They visited us once on Lasqueti? Two daughters, a little younger than you?"

I nodded. "Sort of. Is one of them black? And has really big hair?"

"That's Mary." Mom laughed. "I'd forgotten about her afro. Do you remember their girls? You would only have been, hmm, maybe six or seven? I was pregnant with the twins. So their kids would have been maybe four and six, something like that."

I had a vague memory of two women and two little girls sitting in our tiny kitchen. Mostly what I remembered was the hair, because I'd never seen anything like it before.

"Damn," Curtis said, and I looked up to see Violet and Ty heading toward us.

"Yours," Mom said under her breath. "All yours. If I say anything, she'll bite my head off."

Curtis rolled down his window, and Violet stalked over, still holding on to Ty's arm. She glared at her father, bristling and ready for a fight.

"Can we give Ty a ride?"

"We've discussed this already. The van is full. We can't take him, even if we wanted to." Curtis looked at Ty. "Sorry."

"He could sit in the back," Violet said. "On the bed."

"Without a seat belt?" Curtis shook his head. "That's not even legal."

"Or safe," Mom put in.

"It's okay, Vi." Ty rubbed his head with both hands. His hair was buzzed so short it was more like stubble. "I'll hitch a lift. No problem."

"You're hitchhiking?" Mom leaned toward the open window. "Where are you going, Ty?"

"Same as you guys," Ty said lightly, like it was no big deal.

"You're *following* us? Across the country?" Mom's voice rose.

"You don't own the road," Violet said.

Curtis put one hand on Mom's shoulder in a calming gesture. "Violet, of course Ty is free to go wherever he wants. But we are doing this trip as a family."

"Fine. He'll probably get picked up by some psycho," Violet snapped. "Not like you care."

"That's *enough*, Violet."

"You care more about a bunch of stupid bees."

"Get in the car," Curtis said.

Violet gave Ty a long kiss on the lips.

"Blecchhhh," Saffron said. "Gross." Behind her, Whisper giggled softly.

All around us, people were starting up their engines. "Violet. In the car. *Now*," Curtis said.

Violet slowly detached herself from the lip-lock and got into the van beside me. Ty stepped back, out of the way of our row of cars, and held out a hand, thumb up like a hitch-hiker. The cars in front of us began driving slowly forward, and Curtis followed.

Violet waved frantically out the window until Ty was out of sight. "If he gets murdered by some nutcase, it'll be your fault," she said.

"That's a horrible thing to say." Mom shook her head. "I can't believe you put us in this position."

"Yeah, well, I can't believe you put him in this position," Violet snapped back.

Here we go again, I thought, and put my headphones back on.

Eva and Mary lived in a small house not too far from down-town Vancouver, but it was rush hour and it took us almost an hour to get there. I didn't take off my headphones until we were pulling into their driveway. My stomach grumbled. I hoped they were going to give us dinner.

"Well, here we are," Mom said brightly. She unbuckled her seat belt, got out of the car and stretched. "Come on."

We all followed—the twins squirmy from sitting still, Violet withdrawn and gloomy, Curtis bringing up the rear. The house had wooden front steps and a wide porch and was painted in shades of bright yellow and blue. The front door flew open before Mom even knocked.

"Jade! Oh! So good to see you!" A small woman burst out and threw her arms around my mother. She had short blond hair tucked behind her ears and wore a long white cardigan over a short pink-and-green sundress. "You look just the same," she said, laughing.

"Eva!" Mom hugged her back. "So do you." She turned to us. "You remember Curtis? And his daughter Violet? And you've met Wolf, of course, and these are the twins. Saffron and Whisper."

Eva opened her arms in a welcoming gesture and gave us a wide smile. "Come in, come in! Dinner's cooking, Mary will be home any time now, and the girls can't wait to meet you all."

A few minutes later, we were all sitting around in an enormous open space that seemed to be their kitchen, dining room and living room combined. The walls were lined with built-in shelves that overflowed with books and games; a well-worn couch and a handful of comfy chairs were arranged in front of a large window, and a gray-around-the-muzzle sheepdog lay in front of an unlit woodstove.

"Tess! Hazel!" Eva called up the stairs. "Come on down."

I could hear their feet on the wooden steps: *thumpety thumpety thump.* The dog lifted his head, made a funny wuffling noise and flopped back down when he saw the two girls appear. Hazel and Tess were small and blond like Eva, and both had long straight hair. Tess was taller and wore glasses, but otherwise it was hard to tell them apart.

"Look at you two!" Mom said. She shook her head. "Last time I saw you, you were about the age my twins are now."

They both smiled politely and looked as uncomfortable as I felt. Adults always make such a big deal over the fact that kids grow. It's weird: what do they *expect* us to do?

"I can't believe we've let so much time go by," Eva said. "Life just gets so busy. Girls, Jade is one of my oldest friends. We actually had an apartment together for a while. In New York City!"

Tess nodded, and I could tell she'd heard this before. She sat down on the floor beside the dog and started petting it, and Hazel sat down beside her. Something about this house— the dog, the bookshelves, the smell of dinner cooking, the coziness of it all—made me feel funny and kind of sad. We'd lived in our last place for three years, but the house had always had a borrowed, temporary feel to it. I wondered if we'd ever settle somewhere or if we'd just keep moving from now on.

"So let me put on the rice, and then I want to hear all about your plans," Eva said.

The front door banged open and the black woman I'd vaguely remembered walked in, shrugging off a long raincoat and smiling around at us all. She didn't have big hair anymore—it was buzzed super short. "Hello, Jade," she said. "Good to see you again. Been too long."

"It has indeed," Mom said. "Kids, this is Mary. Mary, you've met Curtis and Wolf and Violet…These are the twins. Whisper and Saffron."

Mary laughed. "You were pregnant with them the last time I saw you. And I don't think I ever actually met Violet. I remember this one though." She nodded at me and sat down to unzip her boots. "Bright pink raincoat and bare feet, out digging in the garden. You must have been, what, seven?"

I nodded back at Mary. She was tall and dressed in a business suit, and she had dark-framed glasses and almost as many freckles as me. I didn't think I'd ever seen a black person with freckles before.

Mom ruffled my hair. "Wolf remembered you. Well, he remembered your afro."

Mary rubbed her cropped head and laughed again, and my face got hot. I stared at the dog and hoped that someone would change the subject.

Eva sat down on the arm of the couch, beside my mother. "Tomorrow is the big day, right? Your first performance?"

"That's right. We should probably spend some time tonight getting ready. We left sooner than we'd planned, so…" Mom trailed off. "Well, the costumes and props are ready, but the kids haven't even had a practice session."

"I thought we were just handing out flyers and stuff," I said. As far as I was concerned, walking around in a bee costume was bad enough. I wasn't planning on actually *performing*.

"Well, I was thinking maybe the three of you could come out first. You'd attract attention—three kids in costume, flying around. And then I could come out and…"

"Flying around," I repeated flatly.

"Maybe you could even do a little dance, Wolf?"

I almost choked. "Yeah, no, I don't think so." I glanced at Tess and Hazel to see if they were laughing at me, but they were focused on Mom.

"Bees can dance?" Hazel said.

"Can we see your costumes?" Tess said at the exact same time.

Mom grinned. "Yes, they can, and yes, you can." She leaned toward them. "Actually, you'd be amazed at what bees can do. For instance, say a colony needs to choose a new home, and there are a couple of different possible places. They have a meeting—"

Violet snorted. "Yeah. They sit around a table in a boardroom, and the queen bee does a PowerPoint presentation…"

Mom frowned at her. "I'm quite serious. I mean, obviously they don't use PowerPoint, but they really do have a meeting. One bee does a dance to explain why her hive idea is best, and then another bee does a dance to argue for her choice—"

"Or his," Tess put in.

Mom smiled at her. "Actually, in this case it's always her. The worker bees are female."

Tess tugged on the dog's ear. "Huh. Figures that the girl bees have to do all the work."

"Do they really dance?" Hazel asked. "I mean, how can bees dance? What does it look like?"

I wondered if she was picturing them in tutus and pointe shoes. "They just fly about in a pattern," I told her. "I can show you on YouTube if you want."

Mom nodded. "Their meeting can last for a few days, until they come to an agreement, and then they all fly off together to whichever new home they've decided on."

"Wow." Hazel got to her feet and did a little jump, tapping one foot against her other ankle. "I do ballet and jazz," she said. "And I'm maybe going to learn tap this summer."

Tess interrupted her. "My mom said you're going to talk about pesticides, right? And how they're hurting the bees?"

I wondered which mom she meant, and if she called both Eva and Mary Mom. It seemed like it would get awfully confusing. "That's right," I said. I looked at my mother. "You should show them the juggling part you do."

Hazel's eyes widened. "You can juggle? Can you teach me?"

"Sure," Mom said, laughing.

"But not right now," Eva called out from behind us. "Because dinner is ready."

After dinner—chickpea barley casserole, salad and vanilla frozen yogurt with chocolate chips and banana slices—I showed Hazel and Tess some bee videos on YouTube, and Mom taught them some juggling tricks.

"Just start with two balls," she advised. "To get the feel of it. Practice throwing them and catching them in a figure-eight pattern, like this." She tossed the balls from hand to hand.

"See? When one ball is at the top of its arc, you release the other one."

"That looks easy," Hazel said. "Can't you do more than two?"

Tess had picked up two balls and was trying it. "It's not that easy, Hazel. Not if you really try to do it right."

Mom laughed. "I can do five, but then I miss a lot. I only do four in the show. It's a bit different when you add the fourth—you can't do the figure-eight pattern with more than three." She threw a third ball, juggled with three for a few seconds and then, without stopping, grabbed a fourth ball and tossed it up into the air. Caught, tossed, caught. "Like that. See how it changes?"

"Cool," Hazel said. She dropped a ball and bent to pick it up. "What does juggling have to do with bees anyway?"

"Nothing." That was Violet, who was lounging on the couch, reading manga.

I ignored her. "Show her, Mom," I said. "Do a bit of your routine."

Mom started tossing the balls to me, one at a time, until she just had a single ball left. "I start with this blue-and-green one."

"The earth?" Tess said.

She laughed. "You're quick. Yes. The earth." She held the ball gently, cradling it in both hands. "I talk about how for millions of years, there were no humans. Human evolution is just a tiny part of the planet's history."

"We did that in school," Hazel said. "We made a timeline all down the hallway, starting at the office, and people didn't even start to exist until we were all the way up the stairs and past our classroom door. The whole time since people started was, like, two inches."

"That's right," Mom said. "And then, for many years, people took care of the earth. We saw the earth as our mother, and we saw all living things as connected. People hunted and gathered, but no one took more than they needed."

"And then?" Tess again. "Farming, right?"

"Yes. Agriculture." Mom looked at me, and I tossed her a second ball. "We started to farm the earth." She juggled the two balls. "We destroyed animal habitats. Overfished the oceans. Cleared forests to plant crops. Turned grasslands to deserts…"

I threw her the third ball.

"Industrialization," Mom said, catching it. "Economic development. Burning fossil fuels. Climate change. Water pollution. Overpopulation. Monoculture." She looked at Tess. "I'd talk a bit about all of those, in the actual perform-ance. Give examples, that kind of thing."

"What's monoculture?" Hazel asked.

I answered, because I'd done a lot of reading about this for my bee project. "Like in nature, lots of different stuff grows in one area, right? And in the old days, farms were like that. Now it's all one thing—like a farm that is thousands of acres of wheat."

Hazel frowned. "Why's that bad for bees?"

"Because for most of the year, there's nothing there for them to eat, right?" I said, and I looked at Mom for help.

She nodded. "Right. Plus, if you have a huge amount of one thing, it's like a dream come true for pests. So then you pretty much have to use pesticides…"

"And that kills bees?"

"That's right."

"It's kind of scary, hearing it all together like that," Tess said.

"That's the idea." Mom nodded at me, and I tossed her the fourth ball. "This one is a yellow-and-black ball," she said. "In the show, I mean."

"For bees," Hazel said.

"That's right. Over the last decade, honeybees have been dying and disappearing at an ever-increasing rate. And it's not just the honeybees. Indigenous bees are dying too." She juggled the four balls faster and faster. "You know what we wouldn't have, without bees to pollinate the plants?"

"Flowers?" Hazel asked.

Tess shook her head. "Think about it, Hazel."

Hazel's eyes widened. "Fruit?"

Mom nodded. "Apples. Pears. Cherries. Blueberries. Apricots. Nectarines. Raspberries. Peaches. Watermelon. Cucumber." With every word, the balls flew higher into the air. "Alfalfa. Apricots. Pumpkins. Squash. And that's just a start."

"Wow." Hazel and Tess stared at the balls, following them around and around.

There was a long silence, and Mom kept on juggling. "So how long can we keep this going?" she asked. "How long can we keep all these balls in the air before it all comes crashing down?"

"And if they all die…Like, if bees became extinct…" Tess trailed off.

"We'd be in big trouble," Mom said. She stopped juggling and let the balls fall to the ground. *Thud, thud, thud, thud.* We all stared at them in silence for a few seconds.

Eva cleared her throat and shook her head slightly. "But people are doing a lot of things to prevent that, right? And looking for alternatives…"

"In some parts of China, all the wild bees got killed," I said. "And now the apple and pear orchards have to be pollinated by hand. Like, workers going from flower to flower with pots of pollen and paintbrushes."

"Seriously?" Eva said. "That's amazing."

Mom kneeled and gathered up the balls. "There aren't enough people in the world to do the work the bees do."

Finally, the adults retired to the kitchen to drink wine and talk about people I'd never heard of. Violet curled up on the couch with her phone, texting Ty, and the twins decided to watch a video. Hazel put a DVD in for them, and Tess got the Monopoly board out.

"I guess it's kind of lame, but Hazel and I play it all the time," she told me. "And we don't have an Xbox or anything. So, you want to play?"

"Sure." It wasn't like I had anything else to do.

We set up the board, divvied out money and started to play. After half an hour, I was winning by miles, but Hazel and Tess kept lending each other money to keep the game going. And the game play went really slowly, because Hazel couldn't stop asking questions about the bees and tomorrow's show, which both she and Tess seemed to think was going to be the coolest thing ever.

"I can't believe we're going to miss it," Hazel moaned, for at least the tenth time.

"It's really mean of Mom not to let us go," Tess said. "It'd be *way* more educational than school." She stretched her legs out and poked the dog with her feet. He lifted his head and looked at her reproachfully, and she petted him with her toes. "Sorry, Timmy."

I rolled double fives and landed on one of my own properties. "Do you call Eva and Mary both Mom?" I asked. "Or…"

Tess pushed her glasses back up her nose. "I call Eva Mom, and Mary just Mary," she said.

"Me too, now. But I used to call them Mama Eva and Mama Mary," Hazel said. "When I was little."

"I guess Mom and Mom would be confusing," I said.

"Yeah." Tess nodded. "And Mom really wanted to be called Mom, and Mary didn't care what we called her."

Hazel giggled. "*As long as it was polite*, she said."

"I just call Curtis Curtis," I offered. "But the twins and Violet call him Dad. And Violet calls my mom Jade."

"But they're all your sisters?"

"Sort of. Violet's my stepsister, and the twins are my half sisters."

"That's confusing." Hazel made a face, like she thought my family was weird, but she didn't say anything else. She rolled the dice. "Four. That's GO! We play that you get double if you land directly on GO."

Tess, who was banker, handed her the money. "So are you going to do a bee dance?"

My face got hot. "Not in a million years." I looked across at my mom, in the kitchen. She was sitting on a stool in her rolled-up jeans, her bare ankles crossed and her long red hair pulled back in a ponytail. She loved to dance. If she wanted dancing in her show, she could do it herself. I looked back at Tess and spoke in a low voice. "I don't even want to wear the costume."

She sighed. "I wish I could wear it. It'd be so much more fun than going to school."

I pictured Duncan sitting at his computer, and Katie moving around the room, checking in with everyone, and fat old Ginger dozing by the window.

"I wish I could too," Hazel said, tidying her stack of bills. "You're so lucky, Wolf."

I rubbed Timmy's ear. It was exactly what Mom always said: We were so lucky. We lived in a beautiful and peaceful country, we had enough to eat and a roof over our heads, we had education, and we had each other—and all that luck, Mom always pointed out, came with an obligation. *With great privilege comes great responsibility.* That was a quote she had written on the kitchen wall at our old place.

Sometimes I wished I was a little less lucky.

Eight

MOM AND CURTIS slept in the van, Saffron and Whisper got the pull-out couch, and Violet and I had blow-up camping mattresses on the living room floor. Timmy the dog flopped across my feet, which felt nice even though it made it impossible to roll over and get comfortable. The twins fell asleep right away, curled up together like kittens.

I could see the glow of Violet's phone in the darkness. "Are you texting Ty?" I whispered.

"Yeah."

"Where is he?"

"At a friend's place." She rolled toward me. "He's going to come to the show tomorrow."

"I figured." I hesitated for a moment. "Um, Violet?"

"Yeah?"

"I don't want to wear that costume."

"So don't." Her phone was lighting up her face. She frowned, her dark eyebrows almost joining. "Just tell her you're not going to do it."

I tried to imagine it. "She worked really hard on those costumes."

Violet snorted. "Did she ever ask you if you wanted to wear one though?"

"No. But I could have said, earlier…"

"So why didn't you?" Her phone shut down and the darkness swallowed her up.

"I don't know." There was a long silence. "I guess because I think she's right? That we should be doing something about the bees and everything?" I hated how uncertain I sounded.

"Don't you think if she was right, other people would be doing stuff too? Jade's not an expert on this. She's not, like, a scientist or anything."

I moved my legs slightly, and Timmy grunted and shifted his weight. "She says people don't want to admit what's happening because it's too inconvenient. They don't want to give up anything. If all the pesticides and stuff get banned, they'll have to pay more for food—"

Violet interrupted me. "Yeah, but come on. End of world versus paying for expensive apples? You really think we're the only people who'd choose to pay a little extra?"

"No. I don't know."

"Wolf, I know she's your mom and all, but…"

"Don't," I said. "Don't. Anyway, Curtis is just as much a part of this as she is."

She sighed. "Okay. Fine. But Curtis isn't making me wear a bee costume."

"I'll tell her," I said. "Tomorrow."

The twins woke early, as usual, and were watching cartoons by the time Tess and Hazel came downstairs, all dressed for school in matching denim skirts and striped tights.

"Morning, girls," Eva said cheerfully. She was in the kitchen, pulling box after box of cereal out of the cupboards and plonking them on the table in front of me: Rice Krispies, Vector, Cheerios, Fruit Loops, Frosted Flakes, Alpen…"I was just getting breakfast ready for Jade's kids. You two want oatmeal? It's already made. Or do you want the junky stuff?"

"Junky stuff, duh," Tess said. She sat down and pulled the box of Cheerios toward her. "Hey, Wolf. Where's everyone else?"

"Violet's in the shower. My parents haven't got up yet." I eyed the Fruit Loops. Mom would flip, but maybe she wouldn't find out. "The twins don't eat breakfast."

"Really?" Hazel looked at them curiously. "I love breakfast."

"Yeah. Me too." I poured myself a huge bowl of Fruit Loops. "Especially at your house."

Eva laughed. "It's a bit absurd. I swear, we seem to collect cereal."

"Where's Mary?" I asked.

"Already left for work."

"What does she do?"

"She works at a health clinic downtown," Eva said. "She's the clinical manager."

"Do you work too?" I reached for the milk, hoping I didn't sound too nosy.

"She's a psychologist," Tess said.

"Well, not so much, these days," Eva said, laughing. "Mostly what I do is make jewelry and sell it online."

Tess leaned toward me, lifting her necklace for me to look at. "She made this, see?"

Twists and coils of shiny silver wire were studded with blue and green glass. "It's beautiful," I said, meaning it.

"I've made one for Jade," Eva said. "A pendant." She put her hand into her pocket and pulled out a small square box. "Want to see it?"

I nodded, and she set the box down in front of me. I lifted the lid off. "Oh...wow." A silver tree, roots and branches spreading and joining to form a circle, and pieces of colored glass like fall leaves, in shades of orange and red. "She'll love it."

"I hope so." Eva put the lid back on the box and returned it to her pocket. "Your mom is one of my oldest friends, Wolf."

"I know."

"How are you feeling about this trip?" she asked. "It sounds very exciting, but I guess it means leaving your school and your friends and all that?"

"Yeah." I ate a mouthful of cereal and wondered what Eva would say if I told her I didn't want to wear the bee costume.

"Your mother is one of the most passionate people I've ever known," Eva said. "She really stands up for her beliefs." She sighed. "Seeing her again makes me realize how little I do these days."

"You seem pretty busy to me," I said.

She laughed. "Crazy busy, with work and the house and the girls. But I meant that I don't do much these days to make the world better. Not like I used to."

I looked at her daughters, eating their cereal, and past them, at the cozy living room, the stacks of books, the half-finished Monopoly game still spread out on the floor, Timmy sleeping on the couch. Their world looked pretty good to me, and a big part of me wished I could just stay here. But if Mom was right, all this coziness would be no protection from what the future held.

They'd starve and die along with everyone else.

Mom and Curtis finally got up, long after Tess and Hazel had left for school and I had finished my third bowl of Fruit Loops. I waited until they'd had a coffee and Mom had been given her necklace before I raised the subject of today's show.

"So what time do we have to be downtown?" I asked. "At the art gallery?"

Mom shrugged. "It's not scheduled or anything. It doesn't really matter."

"Did you put it on the website?"

"Just said *around lunchtime*. I figured there'd be more people around then."

I nodded. "That makes sense." I could hear Violet's voice in my ear saying, *Just tell her*. "Um, I know I'm keeping an eye on the twins and that we're handing out flyers and stuff…"

"That's the plan," Mom said.

"Yeah. I just wondered…maybe I could do that without wearing a costume." I couldn't look at her as I said it.

"Oh, Wolf…" She sounded disappointed.

"I just feel kind of funny about it."

"You'll be fine once we get started."

"Yeah, I guess, maybe. But—"

"Look, just try it, okay? For today's show." Mom tilted her head to one side, her fingers touching the silver tree that hung around her neck. "You'll look adorable, and the three of you will really help draw a crowd."

The *twins* would look adorable, I thought. *I* would look ridiculous.

"Be brave," Mom said. "We have to be warriors, Wolf. Imagine you are a warrior going into battle—"

"In a bee costume?"

"—and you have to face down your own fears. You have to be strong. You're fighting for a cause, Wolf. You're fighting for the future."

I swallowed. "Okay."

She hugged me and ruffled my hair. "That's my boy."

I was almost as tall as her now. Over her shoulder, I could see Violet looking at me. She shook her head but didn't say a word. She didn't have to: I could tell she thought I was pathetic.

Violet would make a good warrior, I thought. So would Saffron.

Whisper and me though? I didn't think we were cut out to be warriors.

Nine

I STOOD IN front of the bathroom mirror, studying my reflection. Black leggings, way too tight. They looked like something Violet would wear. A short-sleeved black-and-yellow-striped top, which was supposed to be loose but which was, in fact, also too tight. I turned sideways, sucking my stomach in. Ugh. I had wire-and-mesh wings jutting from my shoulder blades. The costume looked stupid. No—*I* looked stupid. Bumblebee meets giant marshmallow.

I picked up the antennae headband from the counter. Mom had said she would put the antennae on a hood, instead of a headband like the twins had, but I guessed she'd forgotten. I held it in my hand. A black velvet-covered plastic headband. A girl's headband. With antennae.

I couldn't do it.

My heart was racing, and I felt like I might lose it or explode or something. Without letting myself think about what I was doing, I opened the cupboard under the sink and shoved the headband behind the extra shampoo bottles and toilet-paper rolls.

I never wanted to see it again.

In the living room, the twins were posing while Eva snapped pictures. "You guys look adorable," she told them. Their costumes were basically the same as mine, except that they had gauzy yellow tutus flaring out from their skinny hips.

I cleared my throat. "Um, I'm ready to go."

Eva turned to look at me. "Wolf! Um, did you want to…" She gestured at the twins, standing side by side with their arms in the air like they were flying. "Shall I take one of all three of you?"

"No, that's okay," I said, at exactly the same time as my mother said, "Yes, Eva, take one of them all for the website!"

Eva lifted her camera, but I held up a hand in front of my face. "I don't really want to be on the website."

"Oh come on," Mom said.

"No. Not in this…" I gestured down at myself. "Not in this costume."

"Why not?"

"I look stupid," I said. I was glad Tess and Hazel were at school.

"You look fine," Mom said. "Just get one shot of the three of them, Eva."

"Jade…" Eva put the camera down on the coffee table.

"Or no, wait. I'll put my costume on and we'll do one of the four of us." She headed for the back door. "It's in the van. I'll be right back."

"What about Curtis?" Eva asked. "No costume for him?"

Mom paused in the doorway, looked back over her shoulder and made a face. "He's more of a behind-the-scenes kind of guy."

"Me too," I said, but Mom was already gone.

Eva looked at me. "You okay, kiddo?"

"Yeah." I couldn't look at her. "Fine."

"When I was your age, there was no way I could have done what you're doing," she said. "Seriously. I was way too self-conscious. So kudos to you, Wolf."

"Not like I have much choice," I muttered.

"Sure you do. Jade's not going to make you do anything you don't want to do." She tilted her head. "Right?"

I shrugged. "Yeah. I guess."

Eva looked like she was about to say something else, but Saffron tugged on her arm and she turned away. I sat down on the couch, holding a cushion against my stomach. The shirt was so snug that you could see the indentation where my belly button was.

A minute later Mom came flying back in. She was wearing black-and-yellow-striped tights, a short black skirt and a black top with long dangly sleeves. Wire-stiff wings fanned out behind her, and two long black antennae stuck up from the top of her head.

"Yowza," Violet said. "That's quite the outfit, Jade."

Mom spun around, showing off. "What do you think, Eva?"

"Gorgeous. And you'll certainly attract attention," Eva said.

"That's the idea," Mom said. She held her arms out. "Come on, kids. Photo time."

The twins were at her side in a heartbeat. I stood up, crossed the room and positioned myself behind them, so that I'd only be visible from the chest up. Mom smiled at me. I gave her a halfhearted smile back.

At least she hadn't noticed that I wasn't wearing the antennae headband.

Ten

SHORTLY AFTER NOON, Curtis dropped us all off in front of the Vancouver Art Gallery. I was carrying a canvas bag full of flyers to hand out. We'd printed them out three to a page and cut them apart. You could tell which ones the twins had cut because they were a little wonky. There was a picture of a bee in flight at the top, and our website link at the bottom. In between was a long list of facts about what was happening to the bees.

"Over here, I think," Mom said. She had a bag of props with her juggling stuff in it and a couple of big poster boards. "Let's set up right here." She gestured at the large paved area where we were standing, at the base of a flight of wide stone steps.

I looked up at the two huge stone lions that seemed to guard the gallery and at the big pillars by the gallery doors. "Are we allowed to?"

"Wolf, really?" She laughed. "Such a rule follower."

She made it sound like a bad thing. "I just wondered," I said.

"Yeah, it'll be fine," she said. "There are lots of protests here—the steps are famous for it."

"Okay." I handed a bunch of flyers to Saffron and a bunch to Whisper. Saffron promptly dropped hers, and the wind caught them and started blowing them down the sidewalk. I muttered a rude word under my breath and took off after the flying papers. By the time I'd managed to chase them down, Mom and Violet had the poster-board display all set up, and a couple of curious pedestrians had stopped to see what we were up to.

"Here," I told Saffron, returning her flyers to her. "Hold on tight, okay?"

She nodded, pink cheeked from the chilly breeze. Beside her, twisting the flyers in her hand, Whisper looked wide-eyed and frightened.

"Just stay together, okay?" I told them. "And don't go anywhere—Whisper, quit crumpling the papers—just stay right here. Probably no one is even going to come and watch anyway." Curtis was supposed to come back for us at two o'clock—he was going to drive around to a bunch of Chinese restaurants and collect used cooking oil to fuel the van—and I wondered what we'd do for two hours if no one showed up. Would Mom do her whole show anyway, juggling routine and all? Or would we just stand around, getting cold and looking dumb in our bee costumes?

"Hey, hey," a low voice said behind me.

I turned. Ty was standing there, hands in his pockets, grinning at me. Violet spotted him, squealed and threw herself into his arms. "Ty! You made it!"

"'Course I did," he said. "I told you I'd be here." He looked at me over Violet's shoulder. "Whoa, Wolf, buddy. That's quite the look."

I felt a rush of heat to my face and quickly folded my arms across my chest. "Yeah, well."

"Wolf! Violet!" Mom called. "Get over here."

I shrugged, glad of an excuse to take my goofy-looking striped self away from Ty. I beckoned for the twins to come with me and walked over to where Mom was standing with a small group of people. Students, maybe. They looked like students, anyway, in jeans and with bags slung over their shoulders.

"This is my son, Wolf," Mom said. "And my girls, Saffron and Whisper. And over there...my stepdaughter, Violet. Apparently she's busy."

The students all looked where she was pointing. Violet was still standing with her arms wrapped around Ty. Everyone laughed.

"It's cool that you're doing this," one of them told me. She was tall, and her blond hair was tied up in a huge mass of dreadlocks. "Like, as a family? It's awesome."

I didn't know what to say, so I just nodded.

"Well," Mom said. "This is our first show, so you're our guinea pigs." She grinned. "Might as well get started, I guess, though it feels funny performing for six people."

"Go for it." A fat guy with a bushy ginger beard gestured toward the steps. "More people will stop and watch once you get going."

Mom took a deep breath and nodded. I could tell she was nervous. "All right," she said, and she moved away from the group to stand on the bottom step. "We're here because we care," she began. "We're here because time is running out…"

I nudged Saffron. "You and Whisper give out the flyers now, okay? Just hand one to each person who's watching. And if you see someone walking by but kind of looking at us, run over and give them a flyer too."

"Can you do it?"

"I thought you wanted to," I said. "You were all excited about this part, remember? You can pretend you're flying."

"I'm cold," she said.

I sighed. "Fine." I handed out flyers to the group of students. Mom was starting the juggling part of her show, holding the blue-and-green Earth ball in her hands. A couple of young Asian men walked by, eyes on their phones, not even glancing our way. A woman with a stroller slowed down and looked, but when I started moving toward her she avoided my eyes and quickened her pace. Like I was going to try to sell her something.

I didn't want to push the twins, especially if they were feeling shy, but they'd be better at this part. No one would turn their back on two five-year-olds dressed in bee costumes.

On the bottom step, Mom was juggling three balls and talking nonstop. The students were listening, and every once in a while, when she said something they agreed with or did a cool trick, like throwing a ball behind her back and catching it, they'd break into applause.

A large group of people—a dozen or so of them—was approaching. I nudged Saffron. "Come with me, okay?"

She shook her head. To my surprise, Whisper slipped her hand into mine. "You'll come?" I asked her.

She nodded.

"Me too," Saffron said immediately.

"Great." The three of us walked toward the group, flyers in hand, and a couple of young women stopped. "Awww, look at you. How cute is that?" one of them cooed. The rest of the group slowed down and looked at us.

"Go on, kids," I said under my breath. "Give them flyers."

Saffron went one better. "That's my mom," she told them, pointing. "She's a good juggler."

"She sure is," the girl said. She had long dark hair and didn't look much older than Violet. "So how come you're all dressed up?"

"We're bees," Saffron said. "Because we don't want all the bees to die."

"Awww," the girl said again. The whole group had stopped walking now and turned toward the steps, watching my mom juggle. "Are you handing out information then? About bees?"

Saffron nodded and held out her flyers. "You can have one."

More people were stopping now, as if the very fact that the crowd had reached a certain size was enough to make it grow all by itself. Whisper buzzed around the group, weaving in and out of legs, silently handing out flyers. Saffron was still chatting with the dark-haired teenager.

I looked over to where Violet and Ty had been, but they weren't there anymore. On the steps, Mom was shouting out alarming statistics about bees and pollination and our food supply, juggling four balls higher and higher. I spun around, searching the crowd, scanning up and down the street.

Violet and Ty were gone.

Eleven

I FIGURED I should wait until Mom's show was done before I told her. Maybe Violet had just gone with Ty to grab a coffee or something, and she'd be back any minute. I just had to make sure I didn't lose the twins. It wasn't easy, trying to keep an eye on them in this mass of people twice their height.

It was clouding over and a few drops of rain were starting to fall, but even when Mom was finished the show, people didn't leave. They crowded around her, asking questions, arguing about stuff. I tried to catch her eye.

"Where's Curtis?" Saffron asked. "Will he be here soon? I'm cold."

I rubbed her bare arms. She had goose bumps. "Whisper, are you cold too?"

Whisper nodded.

Saffron was right, I thought. Whisper wasn't talking at all.

"Mom!" I called out, pushing through the crowd. "The twins are freezing. And…" I leaned in close and lowered my voice, not wanting to make a public announcement. "Violet's taken off with Ty."

"Oh, Wolf." She looked at me, exasperated, as if these things were somehow my fault. "Look, just keep the girls happy for a few minutes, can't you?" She gestured across the street. "Find a coffee shop or something—get them a drink."

"I'll need some money."

She put her hands on her hips in search of a pocket. "Curtis has my wallet."

I rolled my eyes. "Fine." I walked away from her and her fans, took the twins by their hands and tried to think up a game to keep them entertained. I didn't want to risk hide-and-seek: we'd already lost Violet. "You guys want to play scavenger hunt?"

Saffron eyed me critically. "Like how?"

"Like…" I thought fast. "Like, okay. You two have to touch something green, something brown, something red and something blue. Go!"

They stared at me for about a second, and then they were running. "Grass!" Saffron yelled, bending down and uprooting a handful of it. Whisper followed her, touching the grass and darting across the sidewalk to a parking sign to touch the blue letters. "I can't find red," Saffron protested. "There's no red, Wolf!"

"Sure there is." I looked pointedly down at Whisper's feet in their red Crocs. "Keep looking."

She followed my eyes and squealed, pouncing on Whisper and grabbing her foot. "That's it! I win!"

Startled, Whisper gasped, and tears came to her eyes. I rushed over, hoping to head off a meltdown. "Hey, nice teamwork!" I said. "You guys got all four colors so fast!"

They both stared at me for a second, and then Saffron opened her mouth. "But I won!"

I shook my head at her warningly. "Great teamwork," I said again.

Too late. Whisper sank to the ground, curled up with her arms around her knees and started to wail. "Nice," I said to Saffron.

She started to cry too. "What did I do?"

I couldn't deal with this. Could. Not. Deal. I turned back toward where Mom was standing at the steps, her juggling balls on the ground at her feet. The crowd had moved on; there were just a couple of student types and a bearded older man still talking to her. "Mom!" I yelled.

She looked over. I pointed at the twins. "We need to go," I said. I knew she couldn't hear me, but I just stood there, waiting, until she excused herself, picked up her stuff and headed our way. Deep inside me, I felt something boiling up, like bubbling hot magma trapped under the Earth's shifting plates, pressure building, ready to blow.

Twelve

MOM MANAGED TO calm the twins down. She called Curtis, who came back to pick us up, and we all headed to Eva's house.

All of us except Violet.

"What are we going to do?" I asked Mom in a low voice. The twins were on the couch, watching cartoons, and I was helping Mom make a late lunch for everyone: peanut butter on toast and sliced bananas. Curtis had driven back downtown to look for Violet.

Mom stuck more bread in the toaster. "Hopefully, Curtis will be back with her soon. And we'll head toward Hope. Stop overnight in Chilliwack, do a presentation there tomorrow afternoon…"

"And what if Curtis doesn't find her? What if she's taken off with Ty?"

She shook her head. "We can't stay here with Eva indefinitely. If she's not back by tonight…"

"We can't just leave without her," I said. "Can we?"

"I don't see what choice we have." She pulled a stack of plates out of the cupboard and started placing the banana slices on them, arranging them like two eyes, a nose and a smiling mouth.

"Well, maybe we should wait a few days?" I liked the thought of staying longer—spending the evenings with Tess and Hazel, playing Monopoly, eating Eva's good cooked dinners and the kind of junky breakfast cereal my mom never bought.

"We'll see." She spread peanut butter on a slice of bread, cut it into thin strips and arranged them like sticking-up hair above the banana faces.

"Mom." I hesitated. "Um, do you think Whisper is okay?"

She looked across at the twins on the couch. "She's fine. Can you take these two plates to them? I'll make you a sandwich, okay? D'you want banana in yours?"

"Sure." I picked up the plates and stood there for a second longer. "You know, she isn't really talking."

"She's always been a shy one," Mom said. "Don't worry so much."

"Yeah. But I haven't heard her say anything for days. I mean, not a word."

Mom laughed. "Her sister talks enough for both of them."

I looked over at the two of them, snuggled together on the couch. "She gets really upset sometimes though. Whisper, I mean. Like, those meltdowns she has…Saffy doesn't do that."

"Kids are all different," Mom said. "Besides, you had your share of meltdowns when you were little. Lots of kids do."

"At least I talked," I said.

Mom shook her head. "She's only five, Wolf. Let her be who she is. She'll be okay."

"What if she's not okay though? I mean, don't kids sometimes need help?"

"Kids need love," she said. "And time and space to grow in their own way. At their own pace. Whisper doesn't have to follow anyone else's schedule."

I nodded. "Yeah. I guess."

"And you don't either," she said, ruffling my hair.

I didn't say anything, but it seemed to me that I had to follow my mom's schedule. Otherwise I'd be back at school, drawing comics and writing reports about animals and watching Duncan make computer games.

Though, of course, we were following Mom's plan for good reasons. Watching Duncan muck about on the school computer wasn't going to stop the bees from dying.

Mom gave me a little push. "Now, go take those plates to your sisters, okay?"

At three o'clock, Eva came home with Tess and Hazel and a carload of groceries. I closed my notebook—I was drawing a monster, but its wings were kind of lopsided and I couldn't get the mouth right—and got up to help.

"How did it go?" Eva asked me as we unpacked groceries on the kitchen counter.

"Fine," I said. "But cold. Mom's upstairs having a bath to warm up. And Violet's taken off."

She stared at me. "Taken off?"

"With her boyfriend. Ty."

Hazel was wide-eyed, clutching a bag of dog food to her chest. "Your sister took off with her boyfriend? Do you know where she is?"

"Nope." I took can after can of chickpeas out of a shopping bag. "Curtis went back downtown to look for her."

"What's her boyfriend like?" Tess asked. "Is he cute?"

I made a face. "No. I don't know. He's older. Seventeen."

Eva's forehead creased. "Jade must be beside herself."

"Uh, I think she's worried about getting to Hope. We're supposed to be leaving tomorrow, right?"

"You can stay here. Is she worried about overstaying her welcome? Because you're welcome to stay with us as long as you need to." Eva squeezed my shoulder. "You can't leave without Violet, obviously."

"Right. Obviously."

But I wasn't sure that Mom felt the same way.

Thirteen

MARY GOT HOME from work around five o'clock, and Curtis showed up shortly after—without Violet. We all had dinner together: veggie burgers and these totally awesome yam fries with some kind of creamy garlic dip, and berry-apple crumble for dessert. The food was great, and Whisper actually ate a few of the yam fries along with her usual bread and peanut butter, but there was a weird tension because of Violet not being there. No one talked about it until the twins and Hazel had gone to play upstairs in Hazel's room. I was still at the table, having seconds of dessert, and Tess was doing homework in the living room.

"What are you going to do?" Mary asked.

"We have to be in Hope in two days," Mom said. "And we'd planned to do a show in Chilliwack tomorrow."

Curtis paused, his spoon halfway to his mouth. "Well, we can't leave without Violet."

Mom frowned. "I'm not letting her sabotage this trip, Curtis. She knows what the plan is. She knows we're not staying in Vancouver."

"She has a phone, right?" Eva said. "Is she not answering?"

"I've left a dozen messages," Curtis said. He put his spoon back in his bowl and ran his hands through his hair, pushing it away from his face. There were dark circles under his eyes, and he looked kind of gaunt, like he'd lost weight or aged ten years since lunchtime. "Maybe she'll call."

"You don't know where her boyfriend stayed last night, I suppose? Does he have friends here?" Mary asked. She stood up, unwound a green-and-orange silk scarf from around her neck and folded it neatly. "Maybe his parents could tell us. Do you have a phone number for them?"

Mom shook her head, and I tried to remember what Ty had said on the ferry. Had he told us anything about where he was going? He seemed like someone who didn't worry about details like where to stay. *Ty says we should live in the moment*, Violet had told me once. *He says nine-to-five jobs are for losers. He's not planning on getting old if it means getting boring like his parents.*

"I think we should move on in the morning, like we'd planned," Mom said.

"Without Violet?" Curtis shook his head. "We can't do that."

"She has to learn that she can't just derail everything like this," Mom said. "She can't hold us all hostage."

"Why do you think she's doing this?" Eva asked. "I mean, is it just that she wants to be with Ty, or do you think there's more going on?"

"What do you mean?" Mom asked. "More like what?"

Eva looked at Mary, who shrugged. I could tell the two of them had talked about this before. "Well," Eva said carefully, "I just wonder how Violet feels about this trip. About being away from her friends and missing school…I know Tess is younger, but I can't imagine she'd want to do something like this. And Violet's fifteen, right? That's not an easy age."

"Violet understands why we're doing this," Mom said. Her voice sounded stiff. "She knows how important it is."

"She didn't want to come though," Curtis admitted. "She thinks we're, uh, overreacting. About the bees and everything."

There was a very long silence. Eva and Mary exchanged glances. Finally, Mom stood up. "I'm going out to the van," she said. And just like that, she walked out.

Eva looked at Curtis. "Sorry. I guess I shouldn't have said anything."

He shook his head. "Jade's just sensitive. I think she worries that you two share Violet's views. That you think we're over the top, with this trip and everything."

"I admire you for doing what you believe is right," Eva said. "For walking your talk. It's rare, isn't it?"

Curtis nodded. "Jade's done a lot of research," he said. "She knows what she's talking about. There's plenty of science behind what she believes."

I looked at him. "You believe it too, right?"

"What?" He frowned. "Of course."

"You said *plenty of science behind what* she *believes*."

He looked annoyed. "What *we* believe. Obviously." He leaned toward me. "I was an environmentalist long before I met your mother, Wolf. You know that."

"Yeah. I know." I'd heard all about his off-the-grid solar-powered house and his permaculture garden on Lasqueti. I just hadn't heard him say much about the bees.

"I'm sure you wouldn't uproot your family if you didn't feel it was necessary," Mary said.

I couldn't help noticing that neither she nor Eva had actually said that they *didn't* think we were overreacting. They were being very tactful and polite about it all—but for all I knew, they thought we were nuts. I remembered how Katie had reacted when she'd seen my mom's website, and how Duncan had asked me, "You really believe all that?" I thought about how Violet's mom had called my mom wacky.

A big part of me wanted to jump into the conversation and defend my mom—to tell Mary and Eva how much the bees mattered, and how no one was doing enough, and how they'd all be sorry when everything started to fall apart and disaster followed disaster like a runaway train that no one could stop.

But I didn't say a word. I just sat there and helped myself to more of the berry-apple crumble. Because I couldn't help wondering if maybe my mom might not be right about everything after all.

After dinner I borrowed Tess's computer to check my email. I had a message from Duncan, who was probably the only person who actually knew my email address.

Hey, dude, he wrote. *How's it going out there? School's boring without you. I got paired up with Caitlin for this project we're doing, which sucks big-time. Hey—I read something that made me think of you. These dudes at Harvard have made some kind of robotic bees to pollinate stuff. Google it. It's pretty rad. Anyway, hope you are okay. —Duncan*

PS. I figured out this new way to make the health bar in my game, so now it shows the kill-to-death ratio for each player. I'll show you when you get back. Plus you can slow down time or speed it up. What do you think of Temporal Anomaly *as a name?*

PPS. I'm reading the third book in the Hitchhiker's Guide to the Galaxy trilogy. It's called Life, the Universe and Everything. *Did I tell you that there are FIVE books in the "trilogy"? Isn't that 100 percent awesome? I'd tell you to read them, but I know you don't like reading much, so I won't bother. I'll tell you the good bits when you get back.*

Robotic bees. *Temporal Anomaly.* Hitchhiker's Guide… I realized I was grinning and nodding at the computer like Duncan was actually in there. I hit *Reply* and typed a quick message back.

Hi, Duncan. We're in Vancouver. Violet's taken off with her boyfriend, so I don't know how long we'll be here. We're staying with people Mom knows. They're okay, but I'd rather be at home. Thanks for telling me about the robotic bees. That's cool. And Temporal Anomaly *is a cool name, but people might not know what it means. What about* Time Shift? *Or* Time Warp? *I don't know. I'll think about it. Say hi to everyone for me.*

I wanted to ask him what he thought—what he *really* thought—about what we were doing. I hesitated, trying to think of the right words. Then I wrote, *Duncan, do you think it's crazy what my mom says? Like about the world economy collapsing and everyone starving and all that stuff on her website?* I stared at my own words for a minute. Then I put my finger on the backspace key and held it down until the last part of the message was gone.

Fourteen

THE NEXT MORNING, Mom and Curtis came in from the van while the rest of us were eating breakfast. They looked tired and kind of tense, and I wondered if they'd been fighting.

"Well, Violet texted last night," Mom said.

Eva put down her mug of coffee. "Is she okay?"

"She's fine," Curtis said. "She and Ty are going to meet us downtown today. We'll pick them up on our way to Chilliwack."

I stared. "Them? Pick *them* up?"

They exchanged glances. "Violet really wants Ty to come with us," Curtis said.

Tess leaned forward, eyes wide, elbows on the table. "I bet she said she wouldn't come without him. Did she? Did she say that?"

Mom sighed.

"That is *so* romantic," Hazel said, smoothing her long thick braid with her fingers. "Isn't it, Tess? Like she just can't live without him."

"Right." Mary snorted, put down her coffee mug and stood up. "I better get going. Bye, my loves. See you tonight."

Eva looked at Mom. "This *romantic* thing? You have to know they don't get that from me, Jade."

Mom laughed.

"I blame those Disney Princess movies," Eva said darkly.

After breakfast we packed up our stuff, plus two My Little Ponies that Tess had given the twins and a plastic container filled with cookies that Eva had baked especially for us, and we headed out to the van. I took one last look at the house as I did up my seat belt. It seemed like the last refuge before we hit the road and headed into the great unknown, and I felt sad to leave it.

As we drove, I listened to the silence between Curtis and Mom and ate one cookie after another. They were crumbly and buttery rich and studded with cranberries and hazelnuts and chunks of white chocolate.

Saffron was the only one talking, and she wouldn't shut up. "Where's Ty going to sit?" she asked. We were stopped at a downtown traffic light, and I was scanning the sidewalks for Vi. "There's no extra seat for him."

"Yes, well, maybe Violet should have thought about that before she invited him along," Mom snapped back.

"He can sit here and I can sit on his lap." Saffron giggled. "Or he can go in the back with our stuff. Or…" She started to lose it, laughing harder and sputtering cookie crumbs everywhere. "We could get a roof rack and he could lie on top. Like a canoe."

I heard a giggle from Whisper.

"Very funny," Mom said. "Oh—Curtis, there they are."

I looked out the window. Violet was standing arm in arm with Ty, leaning against the wall of a building near the art gallery.

Curtis pulled over to the curb. "Hop in," he snapped.

Violet got in, taking her usual seat. Ty followed, squeezing past us all and sitting in the far back, seat beltless, on a pile of bags beside Whisper's bucket seat.

Curtis drove off, accelerating with a jerk and squealing the tires. I took another cookie out of the container and hoped Ty would have the sense not to comment on Curtis's driving.

We drove east, past Langley and Abbotsford, and by lunchtime we were in Chilliwack. There were snow-tipped mountains in the distance, and a weirdly large number of mini-golf places along the highway. I wondered if we were really going to have to do a show this afternoon. I didn't want to ask—if Mom had forgotten, I wasn't going to remind her. I snuck a glance over my shoulder at Ty. His hair used to be spiky and bleached blond, but now it was buzzed to a dark stubble.

He saw me looking at him and raised a pierced eyebrow, and I looked away quickly.

No way was I wearing that bee costume with him around.

"So where are we going to park this thing?" Violet asked.

"There's a campground," Mom said. "But it's not cheap. We'd rather find somewhere we can park for free."

"Any side street is free," Curtis said. "But we need somewhere we can set up the tent, so…"

"I'm hoping that when we do the show, someone will offer to let us park in their driveway," Mom said. "And set up the tent on their lawn. That'd be ideal."

"You're going to do a show this afternoon?" Ty asked.

"We are," Curtis said. "You can help."

"Sure," Ty said. "Cool."

"Oh yeah, really *cool*." Violet rolled her eyes. "I can't wait."

Fifteen

CURTIS PARKED THE van on a downtown street and pointed across the road at a low brick building. "See that? That's the office of the MP for the Chilliwack–Fraser Canyon region. Politicians, that's who we need to be talking to. They're just sitting around getting rich and doing whatever big business wants when they oughtta be thinking of the future generations." He nodded at the twins. "Oughtta be thinking about the kind of world we're leaving our young ones."

"What's an em-pee?" Saffron asked.

"Member of parliament," Ty told her. "They're part of the government."

"They work with the president?"

He shook his head. "Canada has a prime minister, not a president. But yeah, kind of like that."

"And a queen," Saffron said. "Canada has a queen, right?"

"Just, like, on coins and stuff," Violet said.

I eyed the empty sidewalk in front of the office building. "We're going to do our show there?"

"Yup. Right in their faces," Curtis said. "Taking our message to those who can actually influence policy. Our government needs to ban pesticides like they did in Europe." He shut off the engine and undid his seat belt. "Let's go."

"Can we have lunch first?" I asked.

"You've been eating cookies all morning," Mom said. "You can't be hungry."

"I am though."

"Me too," Saffron said. "I'm starving."

Mom blew out an exaggerated sigh. "Fine. There are crackers and apples and stuff in here. Grab something quick, okay?" She passed a bag back to us, got out of the van and started unloading gear with Curtis: the poster boards, her juggling stuff, the bag of flyers. I handed a box of crackers to Saffy and Whisper and took a granola bar for myself. Violet and Ty got out of the van, Ty stretching his long legs, Violet bending to fix her hair in the van's side mirror.

"Are we going to put on our bee costumes?" Saffron asked.

"I don't know." I didn't want to put mine on at all. And even if Mom made me wear it, I wasn't changing in the van, that was for sure.

Mom stuck her head in the open driver's-side door. "There's a McDonald's over there. Curtis is going to get the poster boards set up and stay with the gear while we all get changed."

"At *McDonald's*?"

She looked at me. "In the washroom. Yes."

I clenched my jaw. "Can't I just wear my regular clothes like Violet is?"

"Wolf, just stop arguing about every little thing, will you? One Violet in the family is more than enough." She handed me a duffel bag. "That's your stuff. Let's go."

I trudged across the street behind her and the twins. I knew Mom thought I was being a pain, but she didn't understand at all. The costume looked terrible. It really did. It was too small, and I was too big—and it was all very well to talk about being a warrior, but since when did warriors have to wear humiliating outfits?

"Are we getting fries?" Saffron asked as we walked into the restaurant.

Mom gave her a look. "Saffron. Really? Do we *ever* eat at McDonald's?"

"I know, but..."

"No," Mom said shortly. "We are not getting fries." She took the girls by their hands and headed down the hall to the women's washroom, shooing them in ahead of her. "Wolf, you'll be quicker than us, so just meet us back in front of the MP's office." And the door closed behind her, leaving me standing there with the duffel bag in my hand and the smell of fries and burgers all around me.

Mom didn't know it, but I'd eaten at McDonald's a few times, with Duncan. French fries, hot fudge sundaes, McFlurries, baked apple pies. My mouth watered at the thought. I checked my pockets. I had no money at all.

I looked down at the duffel bag. I looked down the hall at the door to the men's washroom and imagined walking back out through it dressed in my ridiculous, too-tight, striped outfit.

I couldn't do it. I *wouldn't* do it.

I turned and walked out of the McDonald's into the cool spring air, almost crashing right into Ty and Violet.

"Hey," Ty said. "What are you doing?"

I looked at Violet as I answered. "I'm not wearing it," I said, my voice low. "I'm not."

She lifted a hand. "High five, buddy. Good for you."

I high-fived her, surprised and slightly giddy. "What are you guys doing here?"

"I'm getting a couple of cheeseburgers," Ty said. "You want something?"

I gulped. "Would you…are you buying? Because I don't have any money."

"Yeah, yeah. What d'you want?"

I swallowed, imagining the sweet flaky pastry and the hot almost-liquid filling of an apple pie. "Are you getting something, Vi?"

"Nah. Not hungry." She looked at me, considering. "You know Jade would flip out, right?"

"I know." I looked at Ty. "I'm good. But, you know, thanks."

"No probs." He winked at me. "Some other time, dude."

Violet gave a long exaggerated sigh. "You are such a wimp, Wolf. Just get something if you want something. Who cares what Jade says?"

Ty poked her in the ribs. "Hey. Chill. So the kid cares what his mom thinks. Nothing wrong with that. Kids should care what their parents think."

Kids. Like I was closer to the twins' age than Vi's. Like I was too young to think for myself. "It's not about that anyway," I said. "I'm just not hungry."

In front of the MP's office, Curtis had set up our poster-board display. It was a three-part thing that stood up on its own, like a kid's science project only way more professional. It basically covered the same stuff as Mom's talk, but in more detail and with lots of scientific references and links to websites and stuff. There was a graph that showed the declining bee population in various parts of the world, and another that showed the dramatic increase in the number of North American bee colonies that were lost every year. There was a long list of possible causes and an even longer list of crops that are pollinated by bees. Scattered throughout, in large bold letters, were quotes predicting our doom: *"I'm concerned more about the death of a bee than I am about terrorism. Because we're losing hives and bees by the millions because of such strong pesticides. We can live with terrorism. We can't live without the bee."—Patti Smith*

Right in the middle, in the biggest font, was this quote: *"If the bee disappeared off the face of the Earth, Man would only have four years left to live." —Albert Einstein*

I felt mad all over again every time I read that quote, because it was wrong and Mom knew it. It gets quoted a lot on the Internet, but Einstein never actually said it. I knew that from when I did my project. I'd told Mom, and I'd even found another quote she could have used instead that basically said the same thing and fit perfectly into that space on the poster board: *"So important are insects…that if all were to disappear, humanity probably could not last more than a few months…" —Edward O. Wilson, biologist*

She didn't change it, though, because she said no one would know who Edward Wilson was but everyone had heard of Einstein. Like that made it okay to lie about what he said.

Her voice startled me. "Wolf, how come you're not dressed?"

I spun around. "Um…" Saffron and Whisper were in their costumes, and Mom too. I felt a sudden rush of relief that I wasn't. "I look stupid in it," I said flatly. "I'll still help, but I'm not wearing it." I couldn't quite believe I'd said it— but the instant the words were out of my mouth, I felt lighter and almost giddy.

She rolled her eyes. "Fine."

I stared at her. *Fine?* That was all she was going to say about it?

"You and the twins can hand out flyers," she said. "Remember that we need a place to stay tonight, right? So if you get a chance to strike up a conversation with someone, keep that in mind."

"You want me to ask people if we can park in their driveway?"

"If you think they might be receptive, yes."

I wrinkled my nose. *Hi, nice to meet you, would you mind if me and my parents and my twin sisters and Violet and her boyfriend used your driveway? And set up a tent on your front lawn? Oh, and can all seven of us borrow your bathroom?* I couldn't imagine.

Then again, five minutes ago I couldn't imagine refusing to wear the bee costume.

Mom's voice was sharp. "If we have to pay forty bucks a night for camping, we're going to be out of money before we get halfway across the prairies."

I swallowed. "Really? I mean, really out of money? What would we do?"

She shrugged. "We'll be fine, Wolf. We can always park at a Walmart or something. I'm just saying we can't afford not to ask, that's all. So if someone seems friendly and interested…well, it doesn't hurt to try, right? They can always say no."

Sixteen

THERE WASN'T MUCH of an audience for the show in Chilliwack. No one came out of the MP's office to watch, even though Saffy and Whisper and I went inside with our flyers. There were two older women sitting behind desks, and a man using a photocopier, and we invited them all to come and learn more about the bees. They were friendly enough and took our flyers, but they said they were busy. *Too busy to care about everyone starving to death?* That was what I wanted to say. It's what Mom would have said. But all I actually said was, "Oh, okay. Um, thanks anyway."

I didn't bother asking them if we could park in their driveways.

Back out on the sidewalk, Mom did her show for an audience of four: an older woman with one of those wheeled shopping bags, a young dad jiggling a stroller back and forth, and a couple of kids a bit younger than me, who rode off on their bikes as soon as she stopped juggling. Violet and Ty sat on a brick wall a short distance away, drinking out of giant McDonald's cups. The twins went and joined them, Saffron climbing onto Ty's lap. Curtis was across the street, the hood of the van propped open, fussing over the engine, which was, he said, overheating.

Even Mom seemed a bit disheartened as she packed up. The young father, whose baby had finally fallen asleep, helped her fold up the poster-board display and carry it to the van.

"Thanks so much," she told him.

"No problem." He turned to leave.

"Oh! I was wondering…" Mom touched his arm. "I don't suppose you have a driveway we could park in tonight?"

He looked a bit taken aback. "Uh, no. No, I live in an apartment building. No driveway."

I could feel my cheeks getting hot. Did he think we were homeless? I guess we kind of were, unless you counted the storage locker, but I wanted to explain that it was just temporary.

Mom shrugged it off. "Right, right," she said. "No worries. Thanks anyway."

He nodded and headed off down the sidewalk, pushing the stroller at a brisk pace. Like he wanted to get away from us before we asked for anything else. Mom didn't seem to notice. She was busy packing everything away in the back of the van.

The woman with the wheeled bag smiled at me. "This must be an interesting experience for you," she said. "Traveling about like this."

"We've just started," I said. "This is only our second show."

She nodded. "A long way to go then?"

"Right across the country," I said, my throat tightening.

"My goodness! That *is* a long way."

"Yeah."

"I have a grandson about your age," she said. "Thomas, his name is. He's twelve."

"Me too. I mean, I'm twelve." I wondered if she had a driveway, and what she'd say if I asked whether we could park our van in it.

"You remind me of him, a little," she said. "Of course, I don't see him often. His parents—my daughter and her husband—they live in Alberta."

I nodded politely. "We're from Victoria."

"And will you be staying in Chilliwack for a few days? Or are you moving on?"

"Depends." I took a deep breath. "We need somewhere to park our van and set up a tent for some of us to sleep in. So, um, we're hoping someone might let us use their driveway. I mean, not that you have to. I didn't mean that. Um. Though, you know, if you wanted…"

She didn't even hesitate. "Oh, you can park in my driveway."

My cheeks felt hot. "Really? There's a lot of us. I mean, Mom and Curtis and me, plus I have three sisters…" And Ty, I thought but didn't say. It was already too much.

"It's not a problem," she said. "I had to give up driving last year. My eyesight, you see? So I don't even use the driveway myself. "

"Wow. That's…I mean, thank you so much. That'd be wonderful. Because, you know, we don't have much money, I mean, we have enough, we're fine, but…"

"It's no problem at all," she said. "My name is Anna, by the way."

She had an accent—not strong, just a hint of some other language around the edges of her words. Maybe German or something. Her hair was dark, but you could tell it was dyed, because the roots were showing pale where it was parted.

"Wolf." I held out a hand. "I'm Wolf."

I introduced Anna to my mom and Curtis, and she gave us directions to her house, which was just a few blocks away. It was a small bungalow, with an even smaller front yard.

"We're just going to set up the tent there?" Violet asked. "Is that even legal?"

"Of course it's legal," Curtis said. "Canada's not a police state. We still have a few basic rights."

"Unless you're a skateboarder," Ty said.

I got out of the car. Anna must be on her way, walking. It had felt rude not to offer her a ride, but we couldn't fit anyone else in the van. Plus we had to stop on the way to buy milk and stuff. I looked down the sidewalk and spotted her, a small figure walking toward us, pushing her floral-print grocery bag on wheels.

"I have to pee," Saffron said.

"I asked you at the gas station," Mom said. "You said you didn't have to go."

"I didn't have to *then*."

"Saffron, that was two minutes ago! If you didn't have to then, you don't have to now."

"Yes, I do." She got out of the van and squirmed about in that have-to-pee dance little kids do.

"Well, you'll have to use the bucket," Mom said. There was a special one in the van, with a tightly fitting lid, that we were supposed to use in emergencies. So far we'd all avoided using it.

"I want to use a proper toilet," Saffron said. "Not a bucket. I can't go in a bucket." She looked like she might cry.

"Hold it then," I told her. "Anna's coming, see? I bet she'll let you use the one in her house."

Curtis had popped open the hood of the van again and was poking about with grease-stained hands. Violet and Ty were standing on the driveway, arms snaked around each other, and Mom was leaning into the back of the van, hauling out the tent while Whisper clung to her legs, wrapping around them like ivy.

"I see you found my house," Anna said, walking up the driveway.

Curtis closed the hood of the van with a bang and turned to greet her. "Thank you so much," he said. "Can't tell you how much we appreciate this."

Anna nodded. "You're very welcome."

I cleared my throat. "Um, Mrs...."

"Anna. Call me Anna."

"Anna. Do you think my little sister could use your toilet? She really has to go." I gestured toward Saffron, who was standing nearby with her legs crossed.

"Of course she can," she said.

I turned to Mom. "I'll take her, okay?"

Mom nodded. "Anna, is it all right if we set up a tent for the kids to sleep in?"

Anna hesitated. "I wish I had room in the house, but…"

"No, no. We wouldn't dream of imposing on you." Mom dropped the tent back on the lawn. "And the kids love the tent. Really, they do."

Anna beckoned to me. "Come on, Wolf. And…"

"Saffron." I pushed my sister forward. "Say hi, Saffy."

"Hi." Saffron looked up at Anna. "I like your necklace."

I hadn't noticed it before, but Anna was wearing a heavy cross, silver, studded with gems. She must be religious. Maybe that was why she was being so nice to us. "It was my mother's," she said.

Saffron and I followed her into the house. "You talk funny," Saffron said.

"Saffron! That's rude." I gave her a shove.

Anna just laughed. "I have an accent, yes? I am from Croatia, but I have lived in Canada for more than twenty years." She opened a door in the hallway and patted Saffron's head. "My daughter wasn't much older than you when we came here. There you go—there's the bathroom. Go ahead, dear."

Seventeen

ANNA LED ME into the living room. "Sit, sit."

I perched on the edge of the couch, waiting and feeling awkward. Anna and I stared at each other. It was weird, being in a stranger's house.

"Um, it's really nice of you," I said. "I mean, letting us park here and letting my sister use your toilet and everything."

"Beautiful little girls, your sisters. How old? Five and six?"

"Five. They're twins."

"The little one...Whisper, is it?" Anna tilted her head.

"Yeah. Well, Juniper, really. Whisper's just a nickname."

She nodded. "It suits her. Quiet little thing."

I swallowed. "She's never been a big talker."

"Well, we're all different, aren't we?"

"Um. I'm kind of worried about her. Actually..." My heart was racing. I knew Mom wouldn't like me talking about this with a stranger.

"Are you?"

"She just gets upset a lot. Tantrums, you know?"

Anna laughed softly. "My daughter—Thomas's mom— she used to have terrible tantrums. When she was three, four…she'd throw herself down on the ground and kick and scream like a crazy thing. One time, she must have been three because we were living in that third-floor apartment in Dubrovnik, she got so angry. She wanted something… I think it was water that had spilled, but she wanted that exact same water back. Not a refill. Not different water."

I laughed. "That's totally something the twins would do."

"She was lying on the ground and kicking her legs and shouting…And I had just had enough, so I walked away. And you know what she did? She just shut off the tantrum, toddled after me and threw herself back down and picked right up again. She looked out of control, but she could just shut it right off. The little monkey."

I laughed, but I was thinking about Whisper. "My sister…I don't think she's like that. I think she gets really scared or something. Overwhelmed. And she doesn't shout." I looked down at my socks. They were stained and grubby. I curled my toes under to hide a hole in one of them. "She doesn't even talk."

Anna frowned. "Not at all?"

I studied the pale-blue carpet under my feet. "Yeah. I mean, no. Not at all."

She shook her head. "Tch, tch. Your poor mother. She must be worried."

"I guess," I said. "But she's so busy with this project, you know? Her shows and everything…"

"Well, you talk to her," Anna said. "All right, Wolf? You let her know you're worried. It's not good to hide your worries."

"I think we're leaving in the morning," I said. "Driving to Hope."

"To do another show?"

"Yeah," I said. "That's right."

"Well, maybe you could take a little break," she said. "Stay an extra day. I bet the little girls could use some fun and exercise. There's a swimming pool a few blocks away."

"I'll ask my mom," I said.

But I already knew what the answer would be. Fun and exercise and swimming pools didn't rank too high when you weighed them against saving the world.

And I could see in my mind a map of Canada, the highway stretching from coast to coast, and along the way a thousand stops, a thousand stupid shows, a thousand black-and-yellow bee-shaped dots.

From down the hall, I heard the toilet flush and the door open and slam shut. Saffron never did anything quietly. "Wolf?" she called out.

"Right here," I called back. "In the living room."

Saffron skipped into the living room, humming, and stopped abruptly when she saw Anna. "Oh. Hi."

Anna smiled at her. "I like your bee costume," she said.

Saffron gave a twirl. "Yup. Me too."

"And so you are traveling around, talking to people about bees? I bet you're learning a lot of interesting things."

I wondered what Anna really thought. Probably figured we were all crazy. Maybe she felt sorry for us. That was probably why she let us use her driveway.

"Ty's telling me a story about a bee called Buzzy," Saffron announced proudly. "He's making it up just for me, but Whisper listens too. Buzzy likes to—"

I interrupted before she could start relaying the Buzzy story in every last boring detail. "Thanks so much, Anna. For letting Saffron use the bathroom and everything." I took Saffy's hand. "Come on," I said, tugging her toward the front door.

"Bye, Anna!" Saffron said, like they were old friends. "See you later!"

Eighteen

THAT EVENING, AFTER Mom had tucked the twins into bed in the back of the van, I asked her about swimming the next day.

Mom shook her head. "I'd like to be on the road by nine. It's a short drive to Hope, less than an hour. We can do a morning show there and be in Kamloops in time for a late-afternoon show."

"Two shows?" I made a face.

"We're going to be doing two shows most days, if possible. The whole point of this trip is to reach as many people as possible."

"I get that, Mom. I just think the twins could use a break."

"A break, already? We've only just started." She tilted her head to one side, studying me. "Are you sure this is about the girls, Wolf? Because you're the only one I hear complaining."

"Yeah, actually I don't even like swimming. But in case you haven't noticed, Whisper hasn't even spoken since we left home. Not. One. Word."

"She's fine," Mom said dismissively.

"She's not," I said. "And I think these shows are really hard on her. Seriously, Mom. All the pressure? It's killing her." I had a mental image of the health bars Duncan had been making in his computer game—a little row of hearts hovering above Whisper's head, slowly disappearing one show at a time.

"She's always been quiet," Mom said. "You can't compare her to Saffron. They're two different people."

"I know," I said. "You always say that. But it's not normal for a kid to go for days without speaking at all."

Mom stood up and put her hands on her hips. "Well, Wolf, if we don't save the bees, her speech will be the least of her concerns."

I just stood there for a few seconds, staring at her. It was like there was this thick glass wall between us, and everything I was saying was bouncing right off it.

She wasn't even hearing me.

In the morning, we packed up the tent and piled back into the van. Violet wrinkled her nose and opened her window. "Wherever we stay tonight, there better be showers," she said.

I tried to breathe shallowly. The van stank of sour milk and stinky feet and French-fry grease.

Anna came outside to wave goodbye. "Bye," I called out. "Thanks for everything, Anna!"

Anna waved. "Good luck!" she said. "Stay safe."

Curtis nodded and gave her a thumbs-up and turned the key in the ignition.

Ka-thunk.

He groaned and tried again.

Ka-ka-ka-ka-thunk.

"What's wrong with it?" Mom asked.

"How should I know?" Curtis snapped. *Ka-ka-ka-ka-ka...* He swore loudly, and I looked at Anna, hoping she hadn't heard.

"You're the mechanic," Mom said.

"Yeah. Right. I'm not a mechanic, Jade."

"Not *technically*. I just meant the van's your department."

He turned to her, his voice tight as a fist. "This is my fault? Is that what you're saying?"

"Don't twist my words. I just thought you might know, that's all."

"Well, I don't." He got out of the van and opened the hood. We all sat there, and I held my breath. The air felt thick with tension.

"Uh, maybe I could take a look with him," Ty said. "You think?"

"Be my guest," Violet said.

Whisper started to cry. "Don't worry," Saffron told her. "George will be okay."

"Look, Mom, maybe I should take the twins and..."

"Fine," Mom said. "Don't go far. Hopefully, this won't take long."

Nineteen

"WHISPER'S TUMMY HURTS," Saffron told me. We were sitting on the lawn, watching Curtis and Ty gazing into the engine like it was a crystal ball. I had a feeling neither of them really had a clue.

I looked at Whisper, who was crying quietly and chewing on a lock of her hair. "Does it? Does your tummy hurt, Whisper?"

She turned her face away from me.

"Saffy?" I nudged her.

"Yeah?"

"Has Whisper said anything to you?"

She shook her head. "She doesn't talk anymore. I *told* you."

"I know. I just thought…How do you know her tummy hurts?"

Saffron looked at me like I was dumb. "Because her tummy always hurts when they argue. Mom and Dad.

She doesn't like that. Or if she has to go somewhere, like school or something." She wrapped her own arms around her middle and squeezed herself. "And she goes like *this*."

"Maybe we should take her to see a doctor," I said. I couldn't imagine how I'd talk Mom into that. She thought doctors were best avoided.

Curtis straightened, walked around to the passenger window and talked to Mom. She got out of the car and walked over to where we were sitting. "Well," Mom said. "It looks like we're stuck."

"Oh dear," Anna said.

Mom gave her an apologetic sort of smile. "I'm afraid we're going to have to impose on your hospitality for a little longer."

"You're very welcome to stay," Anna said. "Very welcome." She clapped her hands together. "Oh! Perhaps you can go swimming after all. Or there is a nice park, just down the street…"

"Swimming!" Saffron said. "Please, Mom? Can we?"

"We'll see," Mom said. "Hopefully Curtis will get the van running by lunchtime."

"Whisper wants to swim too," Saffron said.

"I said, we'll see."

"I am sorry," Anna said. "I'm afraid I have caused an upset."

"Not at all," Mom said stiffly. I could tell she was annoyed though.

Curtis walked over to join us on the lawn. "Anna, is there a garage nearby? Somewhere I might be able to get an engine part?"

"There's a Canadian Tire," she said. "Not too far away. On Vedder Street."

He nodded. "Saw that yesterday, come to think of it. Thanks, Anna." He turned to us. "Well, gang, looks like you'll have to find a way to amuse yourselves for a few hours."

"Swimming!" Saffron shouted.

I looked at Mom hopefully. "If we're stuck here anyway…"

She got to her feet and brushed grass off her butt.

"Ty and me are going into town," Violet said.

Mom put her hands on her hips. "Can we just remember why we are here, please?"

"Uh, because the van won't start?" Violet said.

"This whole trip." Mom sounded angry. "Why are we doing this?"

"For the bees," Saffron said.

"That's right. So why, as soon as one little thing goes wrong, are you all forgetting about that?"

There was a long silence. Anna looked uncomfortable. "Ah, perhaps I'll just…" Her voice trailed off, and she backed away from us, turned and walked into the house.

"We're not forgetting," I said.

"I told Dad not to get a stupid Ford," Violet said.

Saffron put her hands on her hips. "George isn't stupid."

Whisper ran over to the van and climbed inside, banging the door closed behind her. Back home, she would have run to her room. The van was the closest thing she had to a bedroom now. It was the closest thing we had to a home.

No wonder she was upset that it was broken.

"The point is," Mom said, "that if we're stuck here, we should make the most of our time."

It seemed to me that taking the twins swimming would be a very good use of our time, but I knew that wasn't what she meant. "You want to do another show?" I said.

"Why not? We hardly spoke to anyone yesterday."

"Where though? I mean, we can't drive…"

Mom pointed down the street. "We're within walking distance of a high school. I looked online; it's only a few blocks. And young people, well, who better to be talking to, right? They'll be the decision makers in just a few years' time."

"Count me out," Violet said resolutely. "Ty and I will meet you back here."

"That is not acceptable, Violet." Mom's voice got louder. "You are a part of this family whether you like it or not."

"I'm not even in the show," Violet said furiously. "What difference does it make?"

Ty put an arm around her. "It's okay, Vi. We can go, right? Why not?"

Violet whirled on him. "Because it's embarrassing, that's why! Have you seen her costume, Ty?"

He shrugged. "It's cool. She looks good."

Violet snorted and turned her back on him. "Whatever."

"I'm not wearing my costume," I said. "Not at the high school. No way."

Mom shook her head like I was completely hopeless. "Can you help your sisters get dressed at least?" she said. "Or is that too much to ask?"

I looked down at Saffron, whose lower lip jutted out in stubborn disappointment, and then at the van, where Whisper was presumably still sobbing in her seat. "Yeah," I said. "Fine."

Sometimes I thought Mom was so focused on the stupid bees that she didn't see anything else at all.

I MANAGED TO get Whisper out of the van, but there was no way I could get her into her costume. As soon as she saw it, she melted down all over again, collapsing in a sobbing heap on the lawn. Mom and Violet had gone to take turns in Anna's shower, and Ty was playing some game with Saffron on the lawn. He was good with the twins. I wouldn't have expected him to be, but he was.

I pulled Whisper onto my lap and rocked her back and forth. "Hush, hush," I said. "It's okay. You wanted to go swimming, didn't you?"

She nodded and stuck her thumb in her mouth, her sobs slowly subsiding.

"And you don't want to put your costume on?"

She nodded again.

"I thought you liked your costume," I said. "You know? The wings and all? It's pretty cute."

Her eyes were still teary, but she gave me a tiny smile, the corners of her mouth lifting around her wet thumb.

"You do like it? But you don't want to do a show now?"

Whisper ducked her head, hiding her face against my shoulder. I squeezed her tightly, feeling her sharp little shoulder blades and the bumps of her spine. "I'll tell Mom you need a break, okay? It's okay, kiddo. Don't worry so much." My stomach twisted as I said the words.

If I couldn't stop worrying, how could I expect Whisper to?

Finally Violet came out, her hair wet and combed, and behind her, Mom, in her stripes and antennae. Saffron was dressed, wings and all, and riding piggyback on Ty. Whisper had settled down and was playing a clapping game with me.

"Well," Mom said. "Are we ready to go?"

I nodded. "But Whisper doesn't want to put her costume on. I mean, not yet." I didn't know why I said it like that, making it sound like she'd put it on when we got there. I should've stood up for her and said she didn't want to do the show at all.

"Fine. Just bring it, okay, Wolf? She can put it on over what she's wearing." Mom hoisted her bag of juggling stuff over her shoulder. "Ty, can you help Violet and Wolf manage the poster boards? They're not heavy, but they're awkward."

"Sure." Ty put Saffron down and headed to the van.

"I'm hungry," I said.

Mom looked exasperated. "Grab something quick then. At this rate, school will be finished before we get there."

"No point in getting there before the lunch break, right?" I headed to the van, wondering if there were any of Eva's cookies left. "I mean, there'll be more kids around if they're not all in class."

Violet gave a low moan, like she was being tortured.

Mom whirled on her. "Enough," she snapped. "Enough."

"Jeez," Violet said. "Don't have a canary."

I ducked into the van and rummaged through the food bags, coming up with an apple and a granola bar. I slipped the bar into my pocket for later and bit into the apple. It was too soft. I hate soft apples.

Ty handed me a piece of the display to carry, and Violet took another. Ty took the middle piece, which was the heaviest, and we headed off down the street.

"Piggyback?" Saffron asked Ty.

He shook his head. "Can't, kiddo." He lifted his sign. "See? Gotta carry this."

Whisper grabbed Saffron's hand, but Saffron pulled away. I could see Whisper's chin start to tremble, which meant tears were not far away. "Hey, you guys want to play a game while we walk?" I said.

"Like what?" Saffron asked, her voice tinged with suspicion.

I tried to think of something fast.

"I Spy," Ty said. "I spy with my little eye something red."

I looked at him and grinned, grateful. "Yeah! I Spy!"

Saffron was already looking around. "The fire hydrant?"

"No…"

It was hard to walk with the sign. My knees kept thwacking into its wooden frame with every step. Plus I still had the too-soft apple in my hand. I didn't want it, but Mom hated to see food wasted, so I was pretending to eat it while looking for a bush I could secretly toss it into.

Mom was ahead of us, leading the way at a brisk pace. Like a mother duck with a line of straggling ducklings, I thought, picturing the illustration in one of the twins' books. Saffron was the bossy little duckling that always looked for adventures, Violet was the grumpy one, Ty was the leader, Whisper was the scaredy-duck, and I…well, I wasn't sure which one I was. I was just following the others.

Twenty-One

THE HIGH SCHOOL was more than a few blocks away. By the time we got there, my back was aching, and my knees felt bruised from bumping against the sign.

"Is that a school?" Saffron asked. "It's huge."

The only school we'd ever gone to was our tiny one back home, which was just a converted house. This high school was huge and modern, an ugly two-story building with not enough windows. "It looks like a jail," I said.

"Great. Lock me up and leave me here," Violet muttered.

Ty laughed. "Oh come on, Vi. Your life's not that bad."

She rolled her eyes. "Easy for you to say. You can leave any time."

Mom stopped walking and put her bag down in a grassy area in front of the school. I lowered my voice as we approached. "Violet's right, Ty. We're going to be doing this every day for weeks. Months, even."

He lifted one eyebrow quizzically. "I thought you were a true believer," he said. "Bee boy, right?"

"What?" I stopped abruptly, thwacking my bruised left knee on the sign again. "No."

Ty looked at Violet, then back at me. "Thought it was your research that started all this."

"I just did a school project," I said. "That's all. Did Violet say this trip was my idea? Because it wasn't."

"Yeah, um…" Violet looked uncomfortable. "He did a project, but, um, this trip was totally Jade. She kind of took his bee thing and ran with it."

"Thank you," I said sarcastically. "Because, for the record? This is not my idea of a good time."

Ty nodded. "Got it."

"It's not his fault his mom's loopy," Violet said under her breath.

I wanted to hit her, but we were only ten feet from Mom, and she was already beckoning to us. "Put the signs here," she called out. "We'll get set up and…" She looked at her watch. "The students should be coming outside any minute."

"Right." I dropped my sign and rubbed my numb hands against my thighs. Ty set his center board up and moved mine and Violet's into position on either side of it. Saffron lay down on the grass and stared up at the blue sky.

"Saffron, don't crush your wings," Mom said sharply. "Get up." She looked at Whisper, who was about to flop down beside her sister. "And you still need to get your costume on, missy. Come here, and I'll give you a hand."

Whisper stuck her fingers in her mouth but didn't move.

"Come on, my sweet little bug," Mom said. "Let's get you dressed."

Whisper lay down on the grass, completely ignoring her.

"Whisper!" Mom's tone sharpened. "Enough."

"Mom…" I said.

"What?"

"Maybe just let her be," I said. "I think she needs a break, you know?"

"She doesn't have to do anything," Mom said. She dangled Whisper's costume from her fingers. "Just put this on over her clothes and she can stand around looking cute. That's it."

"Well, maybe she doesn't want to look cute," Violet said.

I looked at her in surprise. Since when did Violet ever take my side about anything?

"I'm doing this for her," Mom said. "For all of you. So that you can have a decent world to grow up in. So you can have a future."

Violet snorted and shoved her hands deep into the pockets of her stretched-out black hoodie.

Mom handed me the costume. "I've got to find a washroom—I'm desperate for a pee. Wolf, get your sister dressed, will you?" She hurried off into the school building, striped tights, antennae and all. I wondered if any teachers would see her, and what they would make of all this.

Violet looked at me. "Jade's, like, totally checked out."

"I know."

"I mean, look at Whisper. She's going to freak if you try to put that on her."

Whisper was sitting on the grass, knees pulled up to her chest, sucking on her fingers.

"Whisper?" I said. "Are you going to put your wings on?"

Saffron flopped back down on the grass, apparently not caring if her wings got crushed. "She doesn't want to wear her costume," she said. "Duh."

I shrugged and looked at Violet. "I wish we could have gone swimming."

"Me too." Violet's dark eyebrows drew together, and the corners of her mouth pulled down in a deep scowl. "This is messed up. Making the twins do this. They're just babies."

"I'm not a baby," Saffron said indignantly, sitting back up. "That's mean to say."

"She didn't mean it in a bad way," Ty told her. He walked over to her and poked her tummy gently.

Saffron giggled. "That tickles."

"She just meant you two should be having fun," Ty said. "Not worrying about grown-up stuff."

"I wish we had a grandma like Anna," Saffron said dreamily. "Who would take us swimming."

I blew out a long breath. "Me too."

"I have a grandma," Violet said. "My dad's mom. We used to see her all the time when I was little. She even lived with us for a while on Lasqueti."

"Really?"

"Yeah. She used to look after me when Dad was working."

"How come I don't remember her?" I asked.

"She moved to Nelson," Violet said. "Before the twins were born. I don't think she and Jade got along too well."

"So she's their grandmother too," I said. "Saffy and Whisper's." Everyone except me, I thought.

"Yeah, duh." Violet made a face. "Curtis took them to visit her once, don't you remember? A couple of years ago?"

I shook my head. "Nope."

"Well, he did. I was staying with my mom. And you were at that dumb camp."

"Oh yeah." It was the only time I'd gone to a sleepover camp, and I'd hated it.

Mom walked out of the school and joined us. "Wolf! I asked you to get Whisper dressed."

"Yeah." I gestured helplessly. "She really doesn't want to. Um, maybe we should just let it go?"

A bell rang loudly in the building behind us.

"Lunch bell," Mom said. "Whisper, enough lollygagging. Come and get dressed."

I could see it coming, even if Mom couldn't. Whisper's face was getting red and blotchy, her chin was wobbling, she was rocking back and forth like she was trying to drown everything else out. "Mom," I said. "She's going to have a major meltdown if you push it."

"Fine," Mom snapped, like it was all my fault. "I'll do the presentation with Saffron. You lot—Wolf, Ty, Violet— perhaps, between the three of you, you can manage to look after one five-year-old?"

Ty picked up Whisper in his arms like she weighed nothing at all and strode away without a word. Violet and I followed. Teenagers were streaming out of the building, looking curiously at Mom and her signs. She started to juggle three balls, smiling at people, gathering a crowd around her. Ty didn't look back. He walked fast, all the way to the far side of the school field, and Violet and I had to jog to keep up.

"It's like she doesn't even see how upset Whisper is," I said to Violet.

Ty stopped walking and set Whisper down on the grass. "There you go, kiddo. Why don't you go play? I bet you could climb that tree there."

Whisper's lower lip was jutting out unhappily, but at least she wasn't crying.

"Go on," I said. "Look at all those pinecones."

She wandered toward the tree I was pointing at—a tall Douglas fir—and began collecting cones.

"Jade doesn't see *anything*," Violet said. Her voice sounded all choked up. "She doesn't see that she's totally messed up my whole tenth-grade year."

I played with the zipper on my hoodie—up and down, up and down. "All she thinks about is the stupid bees," I said.

"The end is nigh," Ty intoned. "Death, doom, destruction…These are the end times."

"Shut up," I said. It was one thing for me—and even Violet—to criticize Mom, but Ty wasn't part of the family.

He just laughed. "Buzz, buzz, buzz."

Violet shoved him. "Enough. You're not funny, Ty."

He was right though. Mom was so stuck on this idea that disaster was lurking just around the corner that she wasn't even seeing what was right in front of her face. I imagined the days and weeks ahead: all of us crammed into that stinky van, driving from town to town, parking in strangers' driveways or shopping-mall parking lots. "This trip was a really bad idea," I said quietly. "Wasn't it?"

"Duh," Violet said. "It's a freaking nightmare. It's even worse than I thought it would be, and I thought it would be pretty bad."

"I know." I wished I was back at school, petting Ginger and listening to Duncan talk about his games and working on some idea for a new project—the history of comic books or Shakespeare or rocket science. Anything other than bees.

Violet turned to Ty. "Screw it. Let's get out of here."

"Sure, babe." He gave her a slow smile. "Where d'you want to go?"

Violet hesitated. "I don't know. Home, sort of, but I guess we don't have one anymore. And I'm not going to my mom's place." She bit her lip. "Maybe Nelson?"

"To your grandmother's?" I wondered what she was like. Someone with Anna's warmth and common sense maybe. Someone with a dog and bookshelves and board games and a busy kitchen, like Eva and Mary.

Someone who didn't think the world was ending.

"Take me too," I said impulsively. "Take me with you."

Violet looked at me. "What about the twins?"

I couldn't believe she hadn't just said no. I looked at Whisper, who was stockpiling cones at the base of the tree. Violet was right. We couldn't all take off and leave the twins behind. "Them too," I said. "She's their grandmother, right? Maybe she can help Whisper. Get her to a doctor or something."

Violet raised her eyebrows at me. "Well, aren't you Mr. Responsible?"

"She's your sister too," I said. "And she hasn't spoken a word in days. And what does Mom do?"

We all watched Whisper in silence for a long moment.

"Nothing," Violet said. "Like, not a single freaking thing."

"Worse," I said. "She tries to force her to dress up as a bee and talk to total strangers."

Ty rubbed his hand over the stubble on his scalp. "Yeah," he said. "That's messed up."

Twenty-Two

WE SPENT LUNCH hour at the school, and when the bell rang and all the kids were swallowed back up by the building like it was a giant vacuum, we followed them inside to use the toilets and then walked back to Anna's house. Mom put everything away in the van, got changed and helped Saffron get back into her regular clothes. Violet and I made peanut-butter-and-banana sandwiches.

"Saffron did such a good job," Mom said. She stroked Saffy's hair. "She handed out lots of flyers and she even answered questions, didn't you, love?"

Saffron smiled. "I told the people about the bees," she said proudly. "And I told them how we had to get the queen to make people stop using pesticides."

I looked at Mom over the top of Saffy's head. Her blue eyes were laughing. "The queen, huh?" I said.

"Yeah. Because she shouldn't just be on coins and things." Saffron lowered her voice. "Mom? I have to go to the bathroom."

Mom groaned. "We just went pee at the school, remember? How can you have to go again?"

"The other thing. You know."

"Oh. Come on, we'll…find somewhere with a bathroom." Mom looked at me. "Watch Whisper, okay? We'll be back. There's a convenience store on the corner; maybe they'll let us use the washroom."

"Buy some milk," Violet said. "And more peanut butter. We're out." She sat down on the lawn, and Ty lay down with his head on her lap. She patted his stubbly hair, and he pushed his head against her hand like he was a cat. "Want a sandwich, Ty?"

"Nah. Not hungry."

Whisper had climbed into the van with her sandwich and was sitting in her seat as if she thought we were about to drive off. I felt like I should get in and sit with her, but the van still smelled like feet, so I sat on the lawn with the others.

I was eating my second sandwich when Curtis walked up. He had his hands buried in his pockets, and he did not look happy. "Where's your mother?" he asked me.

"The store." I pointed down the street. "Did you get the part for the van?"

He shook his head. "They won't be able to get it before next week. Tuesday at the latest, the guy said."

"That's almost a week away. It's Thursday today, right?" I was counting backward. Monday we'd left home. Three nights we'd been gone, and it felt like forever.

"At the latest," Curtis said. "Hopefully Monday."

"So we'll stay here until then?"

"Well, we can't go anywhere if the van won't start."

I didn't think Anna had counted on having us parked in her driveway for that long. I hoped she wouldn't mind. Secretly, I was glad we weren't going anywhere yet.

Mom was not happy with the news. Apparently she'd set up meetings with local politicians in Hope and Kamloops and a presentation to some high-school classes in Kelowna, and now her schedule was all messed up.

She pulled her laptop out of the van and sat down on Anna's front steps. "I have to see if I can rearrange things."

"Do you have Wi-Fi?" Violet asked.

"Anna gave me her password," Mom said, her fingers drumming on the edge of the computer as she waited for it to start up.

"Can I check my email?" I asked. "I should write to Duncan. And Katie."

"Katie?"

"My teacher. I said I'd send updates."

"Hmm." Mom looked like she was only half listening. "Sure, sweets. Just let me do this first."

"Hey, if we're not leaving today, maybe I could take the twins swimming," I said. I spoke quietly in case she said no— the twins were a few feet away, hidden in the tent but probably listening to every word. I didn't want them to get their hopes up and then be disappointed all over again.

Mom nodded absently. "Sure, sure. Good idea."

"Yay!" Saffy's head stuck out of the tent flaps. "Swimming!"

So much for stealth. Saffron had hearing like a bat.

"Can't believe this," Mom said, sighing. "That useless van."

Saffron clambered out of the tent, looking offended. "George isn't useless!"

Mom looked at her and sighed. "No, he's not. Sorry, Saf. I'm just frustrated that we are still here."

"I *like* it here."

Mom turned away from the computer and tugged gently on a lock of Saffron's hair. "I'm impatient to get to Hope."

"To hope for what?"

"It's a where, kiddo. Not a what," Ty told her. "It's a town."

"No, it's not. It's, like, when you want something." Saffron's hands were planted firmly on her hips. "Like if you want to go swimming, then you hope it."

"I'll take you swimming," I said, laughing.

"Yeah, we'll all go," Violet put in.

Which was weird—Violet never willingly did anything with me. I didn't say anything, though, just started hunting through the piles of bags in the van, looking for swimsuits and towels.

A minute later, Violet was beside me, bending her head close to mine. "Very smooth, Wolf. Nicely done."

I frowned. "What?"

"We're going to the Greyhound station," she whispered. "So take what you need. The twins too."

I straightened up so fast I whacked my head on the van door. "Ow—I—really? Seriously? Like, leaving? Right now?"

"Shhh. Yes. Are you in or not?"

My heart was thumping like crazy, and I felt short of breath. "I don't know. Um. Yes. I think so."

"Fine." She started pulling clothes out of her duffel bag and shoving them into a small day pack.

I tried to think what we'd need. Changes of clothes. Whisper's special blanket. The My Little Ponies the twins got from Tess. Snacks. "I don't have any money," I said.

"Ask Mom."

"What? Are you nuts?"

She rolled her eyes at me. "For swimming, doofus."

"But I thought we were…"

"Wolf. Seriously, sometimes I think you're, like… deficient." Violet blew out a long breath. "Mom thinks we're going swimming. That's, I don't know, five bucks each. So ask her for some money."

"Bus tickets will cost more than that." I picked up Whisper's Ritz crackers.

"Ty's got money," Violet said. "And I have a bit."

I swallowed hard. I couldn't believe we were doing this.

"Hurry up." Violet zipped up her day pack. "Before Jade changes her mind and drags us all off to do another bee show."

I nodded. I couldn't imagine what Mom would do when we didn't come home after swimming. When dinnertime came and there was still no sign of us. "Should we leave a note?"

"Yeah, I guess. So they don't freak out. But somewhere they won't see it until later. In the tent?"

Mom didn't usually go in the tent at all. Ty, Violet and I slept in it, and the twins liked to play in it, but there was no real reason for Mom to go in. "She might not find it,"

I said. "I don't want her to think we got kidnapped or something."

"What about in Anna's mailbox?" she said. "Like, in an envelope? We could put Anna's name on it, and she probably wouldn't open it until later."

"She might check for mail when she gets home," I said. "Which could be any minute."

"Fine, you think of something."

I made a face. "I don't know. I guess the mailbox is okay. I mean, today's mail would already have come, so Anna probably won't check there until tomorrow."

Saffron appeared between us, pushing her little body against my legs. "Wolf, did you get my goggles?"

"What? Oh, right. Do you really need them? I'm not sure where they are."

"I need them. So the pool doesn't sting my eyes."

She wasn't going to be happy when she found out we were getting on a bus instead of going swimming. I felt a twinge of misgiving—was this going to make things better or worse? Maybe it was a bad idea...

I pushed the thought away. We had to do *something*.

Violet scrawled some words on a piece of paper and folded it over several times. "I don't have an envelope," she said. "Think you can put it in the mailbox without Jade noticing?"

"I guess so," I said, taking the note from her. "I'll go ask her for swimming money. Here, Saffy—found your goggles."

Saffron took them from me and put them on, pulling them straight down over her head so that her bangs were caught under the seal. "My hair's stuck in them," she said.

"Yeah, maybe you could just wait until we get there," I said.

Saffron stuck out her bottom lip and tugged her hair free. "Ow, ow, ow. No, Wolf. This way I'm all ready."

I had a vision of her wearing her goggles on the Greyhound all the way to Nelson. "Whatever," I said. "Tell Whisper to come on out of the tent, okay?"

"She doesn't want to."

"What? I thought she wanted to go swimming."

Saffron shrugged.

"We can't go without her," I said.

"Why not?" She looked at me, frowning.

I couldn't answer that. "Look, just go talk to her, okay? Remind her how much she likes swimming. And tell her I'll buy you both an ice cream."

Saffron scooted back inside the tent, and I walked over to Mom, the folded paper tight inside my fist. She was sitting cross-legged on the steps, hunched over the laptop. The mailbox was right behind her, on the wall beside Anna's front door.

"Mom?" I sat down on the step beside her. "Um, we're ready to go swimming."

"Good." She smiled at me. The sun was on her face, and I could see the scattering of freckles on her nose and cheeks. "Sorry it's been so crazy today. I'm glad you're taking the twins for a swim—it'll do them good."

I nodded, feeling guilty. "Yeah. I'll need some money though."

She fumbled in her pocket and pulled out a twenty. "Have fun, love."

"We will."

"Wolf?" Mom grabbed my hand as I reached out to take the money. "Thanks for all your help with the little ones. I don't know how I'd manage without you."

I wished she'd stop being so nice. Maybe we shouldn't leave after all. "Mom? Can I just talk to you for a minute?" I lowered my voice. "About Whisper?"

We both turned and looked at the tent. Whisper and Saffron were still inside.

"What is it?" she asked.

I got to my feet. "Just…I'm kind of worried about her."

She frowned. "Not this again, Wolf."

"She hasn't said anything for three days," I said. "Not since we left. Not one word."

"She's always been like that," Mom said. "It's just who she is. Quiet. She's a thinker, not a talker."

"Yeah. But she's not happy. She worries about stuff a lot. And all this stuff—the bees and everything—I think it scares her."

"How do you know?" she challenged. "I thought you just said she wasn't talking."

"I just know," I said.

"Well, if she *is* scared, isn't that reasonable?" Mom asked. "I think that's a normal response when our whole future is threatened."

"Yeah, but…"

Mom kept going. "Fear is more healthy than the denial of the politicians and corporations and the general public. That's what the real problem is. If people were a little more scared, maybe they'd actually be willing to make some sacrifices."

"She's just a little kid," I said. "I thought, since we're stuck here anyway, maybe we could take her to a doctor or something."

"And make her think that something is wrong with her? How exactly would that help?"

I shrugged. I didn't really see how a doctor could help either. "I don't know," I said. "I don't think this is helping though. Making her dress up and everything."

"Saffron had a great time." She pulled her long hair forward over one shoulder and started weaving it into a thick braid. "She loved talking to all the students. And she feels like she's doing something. She's contributing, being part of the solution. That's what Whisper needs."

I stepped behind her, onto the porch, keeping my eyes on the back of her head to make sure she wasn't looking as I dropped the note into the mailbox.

"Whisper's not *like* Saffron," I said.

"It's what we all need," Mom said firmly. "Don't you feel more hopeful about the future, knowing that we're taking action?"

I didn't. Not really. The future was going to happen regardless of what I did, and even though I knew all the bad stuff about the climate and the bees and whatever else, all of that seemed a long way off. Whisper's tantrums and the stinky van and the awful bee costume…that was all right here, right now, and nothing about it made me feel good. "If I was at school, I could be learning more science and stuff," I said, remembering what Duncan had told me about Harvard and the robotic bees. "And then maybe I could help in other ways. When I'm older."

"Maybe," Mom said, turning to look at me. "And maybe we don't have that kind of time."

I stared at her for a moment. She was shaking her head slowly, and her lips were a thin, straight line. I looked away. She wouldn't listen. Not ever. "Yeah," I said. "I know."

I didn't really want to run away. I just couldn't see what choice we had.

Twenty-Three

VIOLET, TY, THE twins and I walked down the street, carrying bags that were stuffed with a lot more than swimsuits and towels. Saffron was still wearing her goggles, and Violet had her phone in her hand, trying to find an unsecured Wi-Fi network to connect with.

"I hate this stupid phone plan," she said.

"At least you have a phone," Ty said. "Mine totally died yesterday."

"So charge it at the bus station," I said.

He shook his head. "No, dude, it's *dead* dead. It was, like, fully charged and then it just went black. It won't even turn on."

Violet was still waving her phone around in search of stray Wi-Fi signals. "I mean, sure, unlimited texting is great, but *no* data? Who has no data?"

"Starbucks," Ty said.

"Huh?"

"No, I mean they have Wi-Fi." He pointed down the street. "I bet you can connect to their Wi-Fi."

"What are you doing?" I asked.

"Trying to find the schedule." She looked at me. *Bus,* she mouthed silently.

"Shouldn't we have done that first?"

She shrugged. "So if the bus isn't here for a couple of hours, we'll go swimming first." She stopped walking. "Got it."

"Come *on*," Saffron said, stamping a foot. Her goggles were so tight that her eyes were squished half closed.

When we got to the Starbucks we slowed down, hanging close to the doors. "Try now," Ty said. "I bet you can connect."

Violet tapped furiously at her phone, her tongue poking out between her teeth as she stared at the screen.

"Why are we stopping?" Saffron demanded. Beside her, Whisper slipped her Croc off her foot and shook a pebble out.

"Got it!" Violet announced.

Saffron squinted at her. "Got *what*?"

"Crap," Violet said.

Saffron giggled and nudged Whisper. "Violet said a swear!"

"Crap isn't a real swear," Violet said. "It's like saying poo."

Saffron laughed out loud. "Poo! You said poo!"

Whisper smiled, her cheeks dimpling.

Violet handed me the phone, and I looked down at the screen. It showed the bus schedule for Chilliwack to Nelson. The first thing that caught my eye was the price. "That's like…" I added up the numbers quickly. "Four hundred dollars. More. For all of us."

"For what?" Saffron asked. "For swimming?"

"The *time*," Violet said, pointing.

I followed her finger. "Oh. Only one bus a day?"

"In the morning," she said glumly.

"Might as well go swimming now," Ty said.

Saffron stared at us through the thick plastic of her goggles. "What are you *talking* about?"

"The note," I said to Violet. "In the mailbox. We can't let anyone find it."

She made a face. "Right."

"What are we standing here for?" Saffron said. "I want to go swimming!"

Whisper's lower lip jutted out, and the skin under her eyes was flushed blotchy pink, like she was about to cry.

"Yeah, we're going swimming," Ty said. "'Course we are." He and Violet exchanged looks.

"Wolf...how about we take the girls swimming and you go back and get the note?" Violet said. "Tell Mom you got a stomach ache or something."

I nodded. I wasn't going to enjoy myself at the pool if I was worrying about Mom finding that note. I didn't know exactly what Violet had written, but I knew Mom and Curtis would freak out big-time if they read it. "Okay," I said. I pulled the twenty-dollar bill out of my pocket and handed it to her. "Have fun."

"Aren't you coming?" Saffron asked.

I shook my head. "Nah. My tummy's not feeling good." I really did have a stomach ache—I didn't even have to lie.

"Here, Violet, take my bag. Saffy's swimsuit's in it. I'll see you guys later."

I sprinted back to the house, slowing down when I was half a block away in case Mom was looking. I didn't see her though. The front door of the house was open, so Anna must be home. Maybe Mom and Curtis were in the house with her...

I stuck my head inside. "Mom?" I called out.

Anna appeared in the hallway. "Wolf. She's not here."

"Oh." I took a step back.

She held up a hand. "You'd better come in. We need to talk."

"What..." I started to ask. Then I saw what she was holding. Violet's note. "Oh."

Anna gestured toward the living room, and I followed, heat flaring in my cheeks and ears. "Don't tell Mom," I said. "Please?" I held out my hand, and she gave me the note. I looked down at it, scanning the words scrawled in Violet's messy blend of cursive and printing: *Jade and Curtis— We've all gone away for a bit because this trip stinks. Don't worry, we're fine —Vi*

I looked up at Anna, trying frantically to think of some kind of lie that would keep me out of trouble.

"Where are the others?" she asked.

"Swimming."

She looked at me skeptically. "Really?"

"Yes!" I dropped my gaze, looking down at the blue carpet, and swallowed hard. "We were going to take the bus,"

I said. My voice sounded funny. "To Nelson. But it doesn't go until the morning."

Anna nodded but didn't say anything. I kept staring at the carpet, which had flecks of gray and white in it. The unanswered question hung in the air: Were we still planning to go? If she asked, I'd have to tell her—and if I told her, she'd feel like she had to tell our parents. Don't ask, I thought. Please don't ask.

But when she finally spoke, her question was a different one. "Why?" she asked. "Why did you want to run away?"

There were so many reasons. Hating the costume, dreading the shows, the thought of all of us crammed into the van day after day. But I could put up with all of that if I had to. "Because of Whisper," I said. "She's stopped talking."

Anna nodded. "Ah." She gestured for me to take a seat on the couch, and she sat on a chair opposite me. "And your mother. Is she worried?"

"She's worried about the future, you know?" I looked at her, trying to see if she understood. "About the bees dying and everything. And it's like…it's like, compared to that, nothing else really matters."

"What do you think?" Anna asked. She was leaning toward me, her elbows on her knees.

"I don't know," I said. "I guess she's right, sort of. She says we need to be warriors." I swallowed painfully. "But I don't think I can."

"And Whisper? Do you think she can?"

"I don't think she should have to," I said.

Anna nodded. "Children should not have to be warriors."

She bent her head and said nothing for a long minute. I stared at the parting of her hair—the white line of scalp that showed between the gray roots. "Are you going to tell my mom?" I asked at last.

She lifted her head to look at me and sat up very straight. "Let me tell you a story. I want to tell you how we came here."

"Here?"

"To Canada," she said. "My daughter was six years old. Just a little older than your sisters. And in my country—Croatia was called Yugoslavia then—there was a terrible war. Dubrovnik, where we lived, was the most beautiful city. Very old, very beautiful." She looked at me. "But then it was attacked by the army—"

"What army? Your own army? I mean, your country's army? Why would they attack their own city?"

Anna nodded. "It's complicated. But yes, the country, it was at war. The Croatians declared independence and the army—the Serbians—they attacked the city. My husband was killed."

"Oh…that's awful. I'm sorry." I didn't know what else to say.

"Yes. It was awful," she said. "After he was killed, I wanted to leave, but my daughter and I were trapped in the city. The army cut off electricity; they cut off water. The city—it is very old, surrounded by thick stone walls, and we were trapped inside. Under siege. Not much to eat, shots and explosions at any time, buildings on fire. My husband was gone. I thought we would die." Anna crossed her arms. "For forty-four days, we were trapped like rats in the darkness. It seemed like the world was ending."

"Yeah." I couldn't imagine it.

"But my daughter was only six. And I had to find a way to keep her safe."

Under siege sounded medieval, I thought. Like something from a long time ago, with knights and castles and trebuchets. "What year was this?" I asked. "How did you get out?"

"It was 1991," she said. "We escaped on a boat. Two thousand of us, mostly women and children. So crowded— six children in each narrow bunk—and the seas were rough. Everyone was sick. But we were free. And then, eventually, my daughter and I learned that we could come to Canada."

"That must have been so scary," I said. It made my worries seem pretty pathetic, and I figured Anna was going to say something about how I should realize how lucky I was.

"It was," she said. "But last year, my daughter and my grandson and I went back to Dubrovnik. For a holiday. It is a tourist destination now. Cruise ships go there. It has been rebuilt—all the damage, all the missiles and rockets—you would never know." She looked at me. "We sat in the square and ate gelato, and I showed my daughter the building where she was born. The world didn't end after all, you see?"

I nodded. "You think my mom's wrong? Is that what you're telling me? That the world won't end?"

"Well, a civil war isn't the same as dying bees." She shrugged. "And no one can know the future. But many times people have thought the world was coming to an end.

And it has not. So I am an optimist. I think things get better, not worse." She leaned close and patted my knee. "And I understand why your mother wants a better future for her children. That is why she is doing this. Trying to make the world better for you."

"I know that. But…"

Anna nodded. "Yes. But she doesn't see what you see. So you have your own battle to fight. You have to protect your little sister."

"That's right." I looked at her, surprised. Was she actually agreeing with me?

"Perhaps there is more than one kind of warrior," Anna said. She stood up, brushed her hands against her skirt and smiled. "Now, shall I get you some cookies?"

Twenty-Four

WHEN VIOLET AND the others got home, wet haired and smelling like chlorine, I filled them in on my conversation with Anna.

"So she's not going to tell your parents?" Ty asked.

"I don't *think* so," I said. "I think she kind of understood."

He raised one eyebrow. "That's pretty cool." He unpacked a bag of wet towels and started hanging them over the van's open doors.

"I bet she tells," Violet said darkly. "Adults always stick together. Doesn't matter who's right or what the deal is, they have each other's backs."

I knew what she meant, but I didn't think Anna was like that.

Ty pulled Saffron's swim goggles from the bag and dangled them from one finger. "So what are we going to do? Violet, you think we should go in the morning?"

Saffron grabbed her goggles from him. "Go where?"

Violet shrugged. "Not like anything's changed."

"So, yeah then?"

She nodded. "Yeah." She looked at me. "Where are they?"

"Mom and Curtis? I haven't seen them."

"I'm hungry," Saffron said. "So's Whisper. And we want a Buzzy the Bee story, Ty."

I stuck my head in the back of the van, rummaging through the supplies in search of easy snacks. "Want an apple?" I grabbed two and handed them one each. "There you go."

Saffron took the apple and bit into it. She was shivering, and Whisper's lips had a blue tinge. Wet hair and a cool breeze were a bad combination. "Why don't you go in the tent?" I said. "It'll be warmer."

"Can Ty come too? And tell us a Buzzy story?"

Ty nodded. "In a minute, okay? You go ahead and get warm, and I'll come in a minute."

When the girls were zipped inside, Violet beckoned for me to come closer to her and Ty. She lowered her voice, speaking in a whisper. "Look, there's a problem, Wolf."

"I've got a couple hundred bucks," Ty said. "And Vi's got a bit too. But it's not enough for all of us."

My heart sank. "You're going without us."

Violet looked at me, one side of her mouth pulled down in an apologetic kind of grimace. "I don't know what else to do. Maybe when we get there, if my grandmother will listen, we can get her to talk to Curtis and Mom. I mean, if you keep heading east, you guys will probably be in Nelson in a week or so anyway. Right? Maybe you can stay there, and Mom and Curtis can do the rest of the trip without us."

I looked at her, trying to feel angry but just feeling stuck and hopeless. Trapped. "What about Vancouver?" I said.

"What about it?" Violet said.

"What would it cost? What if we all went back to Vancouver?"

"What good would that do?"

I shrugged. "We'd be out of here. Maybe we could find someone to help Whisper."

"Yeah." She looked at the tent, and I followed her gaze. "She really doesn't talk, does she? Not at all."

"Not a word since we left home," I said. "I mean, she's never said much, but at least she used to talk to us."

Violet pushed her hair back with both hands, leaving spiky, damp locks sticking out every which way. She hadn't put her usual makeup back on after swimming, and I thought she looked much nicer without all the black stuff around her eyes. "Where would we stay?" she said. She turned to Ty. "You have friends in Vancouver."

He shook his head. "Yeah, but their place is kind of a dive. It wouldn't be cool for the twins to be there." He sucked the ring in his lower lip. "It's not that kind of place. Not kid friendly."

"Eva and Mary?" I suggested. "If we just showed up, they wouldn't turn us away. And I bet they'd understand about Whisper. Maybe they'd even help us find someone who could help her."

Violet shook her head. "Eva is Jade's oldest friend. She'd have us back with her in a heartbeat."

There was a long silence. Finally, I spoke. "What if just you and Whisper went?" I said slowly. "If you took her to Nelson, to her grandmother's? Is there enough money for two tickets?"

She stared at me. "What, you're gonna stay here and explain that to our parents? They'll freak."

"I know, I know. I mean, it's not like I want to." I had a lump in my throat the size of a golf ball. "Um…I know it'd mean leaving Ty. But maybe he could hitchhike to Nelson and meet you there."

Violet made a face. "I guess. But me, traveling with Whisper? What if she flips out?"

"So, you deal with it," I said. "Do you even have an address or a phone number for your grandmother?"

She pulled out her phone. "It's down to, like, 3 percent. Maybe I should walk to the Starbucks and use their Wi-Fi and charge it while I'm there."

The tent zipper slid open, and Saffron's head poked out. "Come *on*, Ty! You said one minute."

"Okay, okay." Ty yawned widely and rubbed his hands over the dark stubble on his head. "I'm coming."

"Can we have chocolate?" she asked.

"I don't have chocolate," Ty said, heading to the tent. "But I have something better. I have…Buzzy the Bee!"

She giggled. "Wolf, can we have chocolate?"

"I don't have any either."

"Curtis does," she said. "In the glove box. He *hides* it."

"Really?" I raised my eyebrows, unconvinced, but I ducked past the towels hanging on the passenger-side door and flipped open the glove box. Maps, Kleenex, vehicle registration papers—and, sure enough, a king-size Caramilk bar and a box of Smarties.

I laughed out loud. Curtis and Jade were always talking about how unhealthy and addictive and basically evil sugar was, and it turned out he had a secret stash. I picked up the Smarties, figuring I could swipe a few for the twins without him noticing.

And there, at the bottom of the glove box, was a stack of twenty-dollar bills.

I backed away slowly. "Violet," I whispered. "Look."

She looked at the box of Smarties in my hand and snorted. "Hypocrite. He's totally a sugar addict since he quit smoking. I don't know why he bothers trying to hide it."

I ignored her and pointed at the money in the glove box. "Not that. This. How much money do you and Ty have?"

She stared at the pile of bills. "He's got two hundred and fifty—something like that," she said slowly. "And I've got eighty."

"So we're only short by a hundred bucks. Less than that." I pulled out the twenties and counted them. "Thirteen, fourteen, fifteen…What's that? Fifteen times twenty?"

"Three hundred dollars," Violet said.

We stared at each other. I could feel my heart thumping, and I had that weird electrical tingling shooting down my arms—that bumped-funny-bone feeling. I took a deep breath and counted off five bills and slid the rest back into the glove box.

Violet nodded slowly. "We'll pay it back," she said.

I swallowed. "Yeah."

So it wasn't really stealing.

Twenty-Five

MOM AND CURTIS came home around dinnertime. They said they'd met with a local member of parliament and dropped off some material for the mayor.

"And then, just by luck, we started chatting to a woman at the library—we were putting up posters—and she turned out to be an elementary schoolteacher!" Mom clapped her hands together. "She invited us to talk to her fourth-grade class about the bees and what we're doing to help them. She was thrilled when I told her about you guys—so inspiring for kids to see other kids taking action!"

"Cool," I said. "So, uh, when's that?"

"Tomorrow afternoon," she said.

I looked at Violet. She met my eyes for a second and then looked away, biting her lip.

If everything went according to plan—if Anna didn't tell on us, if we didn't lose our nerve—by tomorrow afternoon we would be halfway to Nelson.

It wasn't until later that night, when Mom was reading a bedtime story to Saffron and Whisper, that we realized we had a problem. The bus to Nelson left early in the morning—and the twins would still be asleep in the van with Mom and Curtis.

Violet and I were hand-washing the twins' underwear and T-shirts in a bucket. Ty was helping Curtis with some engine thing. "Maybe we could ask the twins if they want to have a sleepover party with us," I suggested, wringing out a small pink top with butterflies on it. It was Whisper's favorite. "If we all sleep in the tent, we could be up and gone before Curtis and Mom get up."

Violet looked doubtful. "What if they say no? Whisper's so stubborn…"

"I don't think they'll say no," I said. "Especially if you ask them. Or Ty. Get Ty to ask them. They really like him."

She smiled, pulling a pair of tiny underpants from the soapy water. "They do, don't they?"

"He's good with them," I admitted. "Violet?"

"What?"

"Nothing."

"Wolf!" She smacked my arm with the wet undies. "What?"

I made a face. "Just…before this trip? I didn't like Ty that much."

She narrowed her eyes. "And your point is?"

"He's okay." I shrugged. "And, um, you know. I'm glad he came with us."

"Yeah?"

"Yeah."

Violet gave a long sigh. "I know Jade and my dad think I'm too young to get serious, but Ty and I are totally in love. I mean, we're always going to be together. I just know it."

"Yeah, okay." I didn't want to get into that. "Anyway, it's nice of him to help us with the money and everything."

"Dad's really going to hate him after this," Violet said darkly. "And when they catch up to us, you and me are going to be grounded for life."

"Mom doesn't do grounding. Or any kind of punishment," I said.

Violet snorted. "Yeah, right."

"Seriously," I said. "You know that. She says kids do the best they can. She doesn't believe in punishment."

"Well, my dad definitely does. And I'll bet you anything he wins that argument."

I puffed my cheeks out and exhaled the air slowly. "Their grandmother—your grandmother—what's she like?"

"She used to bake cookies with Smarties in them, and she showed me how to make those paper snowflakes, you know? And she knits a lot…" Violet's gaze met mine. She'd reapplied her eyeliner, a thick black line that lifted up at the outer corners and made her eyes look like a cat's. "I haven't seen her since I was eight," she said.

"You think she'll be okay with us showing up like this?"

She shrugged. "She'll have to be, won't she?"

At midnight I was still wide awake and jittery. The moon was full, and its light shone through the thin fabric of our tent, making everything look weird and blue and spooky. I sat up and looked around. Apparently, I was the only one who couldn't sleep. I couldn't make out anyone's face, but all around me, their motionless bodies made long lumpy shapes under the shiny fabric of our sleeping bags. It looked like some kind of alien landscape.

I flopped back down heavily. Everything was going according to plan. Anna hadn't told on us, the twins had leaped at the idea of a sleepover party in the tent, Mom and Curtis had gone to bed, and our bags were packed and ready to go. Violet had set the alarm on her phone. Ty had the money in his wallet. On one side of me, Violet lay curled up against Ty, who was snoring softly. On my other side, Saffron and Whisper were pushed up against me. Trying to roll over, I bumped the mound of their bodies with my knee. "Mmm, mmm," Whisper murmured in her sleep. "Uh. Fffff."

It was the first time I'd heard her voice since we left home. I couldn't believe that was only a few days ago. It felt like forever.

My heart felt fluttery, and I couldn't imagine that I was ever going to sleep. I looked at my watch again. Ten minutes past midnight. In less than seven hours, we'd be sneaking out of the tent. In eight hours, we'd be boarding a bus. And by dinnertime, we'd be in Nelson.

I guess I must have gone to sleep, because the next thing I knew, the alarm on Violet's phone was playing the theme song from *Portal*. I sat up in my sleeping bag and looked around the crowded tent. The twins weren't even stirring; they slept as soundly as puppies.

Violet groaned, turned off the alarm and pulled the pillow over her head. Beside her, Ty sat up and yawned. He looked at me, raised his eyebrows and gave me a crooked grin. "So."

I nodded. "So. I guess this is it, huh?"

"Not too late to change your mind," he said.

I looked down at the twins. "What do you think?" I asked him. "Do you think I'm crazy to do this?"

"Nah." He hesitated. "Well, maybe a bit. But I get it."

"You do?" I wasn't that clear on it myself.

"Make your mom pay attention, right? Make her listen to you?"

"I guess so. And maybe Violet's grandmother can get help for Whisper."

"So you're still in?"

I nodded. "Yeah. I'm in."

We managed to get the twins out of the tent without too much noise. Saffron wasn't even properly awake—Ty had to carry her—and Whisper, who was my biggest worry, seemed to accept without any fuss the explanation that we had a surprise for her. We tiptoed past the van and headed off down the street. The sky was a pale gray, and the air felt damp and clammy. Whisper clutched my hand, shivering.

"Don't worry," I told her. "Everything's fine." I think I was mostly reassuring myself, but she nodded as if she understood.

The walk to the bus station took forever. Violet and Ty walked hand in hand, Saffron rode piggyback on Ty, and Whisper and I trudged along behind. With every step, I realized all over again that I was actually doing this.

Running away, I guess you'd call it.

Twenty-Six

ARRIVING AT THE bus station was a bit hard to explain to the twins. Whisper had accepted the *It's a surprise* line, but when Saffron woke up, she had a million questions. Finally, Violet just opted for partial truth—we were going to visit their grandmother. Saffron practically squealed with delight, but Whisper had a big meltdown, crying and holding her breath till her lips turned blue and she collapsed in noisy, gulping, hiccupping sobs. I wondered what she'd been imagining. Some other, more exciting kind of surprise, I guess. Probably one involving fairies or ice-cream sundaes or water slides. Being Whisper, she wasn't telling.

But finally, we were off. The Greyhound smelled different from city buses in Victoria—sort of nice but in a chemical way, like air freshener maybe—and there were actual fabric-covered seats instead of plastic benches. Ty sat across the aisle, eating pretzels from the snack bag on his lap and playing a game on Violet's phone. Violet and Saffron sat together behind me, and Whisper sat with me and almost immediately dozed off. I guessed the meltdown had worn her out. I stroked her head. Her hair was matted, and I could smell the chlorine from her swim the day before.

I stared out the window and watched trees flash past in a blur of green. Nothing felt real: not this road, not our destination, not the weight of Whisper's head on my lap. But for the first time in weeks, worry wasn't sharp and jangling in my belly. I felt weirdly calm. At least I am *doing* something, I thought. At least I am taking action.

It was almost exactly what Mom had said about this whole stupid family trip—*At least we're taking action, Wolf.* I shivered. Did Mom have that jangle in her belly too? Was that why she was dragging us across the country?

I looked down at Whisper, fast asleep, her eyelashes spiky and dark against her pale cheeks, and wished I could know for sure if I was doing the right thing.

Sometimes I envied bees. Not the way they were dying off, obviously, but the way their roles were all neatly laid out for them. Like, if you were a worker bee, you flew around and visited flowers and drank nectar and collected pollen to bring back to the hive, and that was it. You even generated static electricity when you flew so that when you landed on a flower, the pollen pretty much *leaped* onto you. You didn't have to make decisions or think about what you wanted to do when you grew up or wonder whether you were doing the right thing by basically kidnapping your little sisters.

When I was working on my bee project, I'd watched a documentary about how bees used to be practically worshipped in ancient times—there are all kinds of old carvings and paintings and stuff with bee images in them. People thought they were prophetic. If they settled on your roof or whatever, it meant good things would happen.

I've never been a superstitious kind of person at all, but still, I couldn't shake off the question, What did it mean if the bees started flying away from their hives, abandoning their young, dying—or, more often, just disappearing?

I didn't know the answer, but it couldn't be anything good. And I wasn't against what my mom was doing. Not really. I understood why she felt she had to do it.

I just hoped she would understand why I had to do this.

After a couple of hours, Saffron and Whisper were both squirmy and restless. From the seat behind me, I could hear Saffron asking why Mom wasn't with us.

"She's meeting us there," Violet said.

"I want to sit with Whisper."

"Yeah, okay." Violet got out of her seat and stood in the aisle.

I nudged Whisper. "Sit with Saffy for a bit, okay?"

Whisper switched seats, snuggling up to Saffron. I expected Violet to join Ty—he had an empty seat beside him—but she dropped down beside me instead.

"Wolf, we have to talk."

"About what?" It seemed to me that the decisions were all behind us, back in Chilliwack. All there was to do now was sit on the bus until we arrived in Nelson…and then it was out of our hands, really. Maybe Vi's grandmother would help us and maybe she wouldn't, but there wasn't much we could do about it.

"Me and Ty?" She lowered her voice so it was just a fraction above a whisper. "We're not gonna stay in Nelson."

"What do you mean?" I stared at her. "What are you going to do?"

She shrugged. "Ty's got friends in Calgary. We might head out there."

"Calgary," I repeated. All I knew about Calgary was that it had a Stampede and lots of snow in the winter.

"Yeah. His friends have a band, and Ty's pretty good with a guitar, right? And they have a place we can stay until we figure out a way to make some money."

"What about high school?" I said, like that was the most important thing.

Vi rolled her eyes. "I'd have more luck finishing high school in Calgary than I do with Jade and my dad."

"But what about—what about *me*?" My voice came out too loud, and I had to swallow back the wail that almost slipped out with the last word. "I mean…you're just going to leave us? Me and the twins?"

"We'll make sure you get to my grandmother's place and everything," Vi said. She was staring down at her hands, picking at a hangnail, not looking at me.

"But why? Why can't we just stay together?"

"Because I want to live my own life," she said. "I want to be with Ty, and I know my dad and Jade don't like him. And I'm tired of being told what to do all the time."

It seemed to me that Violet had a lot more freedom than most kids her age. "You're only fifteen," I said.

"Whatever," she said. "That's not the point. Ty and I can look after ourselves."

I swallowed. "Promise me you'll still go to school."

She rolled her eyes. "Not much point, is there? Not if the world is ending."

"You don't believe that, do you? Not really?" Violet had always been the skeptic in the family. I counted on her for it.

"I don't know," she said. "Do you?"

I didn't answer immediately. I looked away from her, out the window, at the green trees and the clearing sky, and the sun ahead of us in the east, a golden glow you couldn't look at, not even through the tinted windows. I thought of Anna, and her words came back to me as clearly as if she were sitting right there on the bus with us. "You know Anna was in a war?" I said. "And she escaped?"

Violet's eyebrows lifted. "Seriously?"

"Yeah. She told me that she thought the world was ending, but it didn't. And she said that there's always been people who've thought the world was coming to an end. And it never has. And she said that she thinks things get better, not worse."

"Deep," Violet said.

"Don't," I said. "Don't make fun of her."

"Sorry." She chewed on her bottom lip, and neither of us spoke for a minute.

Then Violet cleared her throat. "It's just…It's hard, you know? Like, I don't really agree with Jade or anything, and I think the whole *world-is-ending*"—she made air quotes around it—"thing is stupid, but still. How do you plan for the future when…"

"When your own parents don't believe you have one?"

"Yeah." Violet's eyes were shining, and her voice wobbled. "I don't actually want to run away, you know. But I think maybe I have to."

My throat ached from holding back my own tears. "Yeah," I managed. "I know. I know."

Taking a ten-hour bus ride with two five-year-olds is not something I would ever recommend to anyone. We switched seats so often it was like playing musical chairs. Ty told Buzzy Bee stories until his voice gave out: Buzzy Bee Quits School, Buzzy Bee Rides a Roller Coaster, Buzzy Bee Gets a Skateboard, Buzzy Bee Plays the Drums. Every time he finished one, Saffron loudly demanded another.

The stories weren't bad, actually. I had a whole new respect for Ty.

But despite stories and snacks and snuggles, after a few hours the twins were losing it. By midafternoon, Whisper had had a meltdown that I thought might actually get us kicked off the bus; Saffron, who never got car sick, had thrown up all over Violet's lap; and a nosy middle-aged woman had asked us too many questions about where our parents were. The time passed so slowly it was like we were caught in Duncan's *Temporal Anomaly* computer game.

The only good thing about that bus was that it finally arrived in Nelson, and we got to get off.

And that was a whole new kind of awful.

Twenty-Seven

VIOLET'S PHONE WAS dead, so we had to walk around searching for a pay phone. We eventually found one at the Walmart, but of course there was no phone book—just the little curly cord that was supposed to stop people stealing it but that obviously hadn't worked.

Violet swore loudly and kicked the wall, and Saffron started repeating what Violet had just said, over and over.

"Nice going, Vi," I said. "I'm sure her grandmother will be just thrilled with her new vocabulary."

"Shut up," Violet snapped. She kicked the wall again. "Can't one thing just be EASY? Just for once, could everything not go wrong? And Saffron? CUT IT OUT!"

Saffron giggled and kept right on repeating her precious new word.

Ty shifted Whisper's weight on his back—she was looking really tired and resting her head on his shoulder—and touched Vi's arm. "Hey. Let's all just chill out, okay? Saffron... enough."

She cast him a mutinous look. She didn't stop, but she lowered her voice to a whisper, which was better than nothing.

"Okay. I'm going to go over to the customer-service desk and borrow a phone book," Ty said. "Violet, what's your grandmother's last name? Same as you, I guess?"

She nodded. "Yeah, Brooks. Diane Brooks."

I held on to Saffron's hand and watched Ty head off, Whisper clinging to his back like a little monkey. She and Saffron were called Brooks too. Mom and I were the only Everetts. Diane Brooks sounded like an old-fashioned movie-star name.

"I'm tired," Saffron said. "I'm hungry."

I looked at Violet. "Any snacks left?"

"Want an apple, Saffy?" Violet rummaged in the bag. "Or...um, a carrot?"

"I want ice cream."

"Yeah, right. Would you like a pony too?" Violet held the apple out toward her.

Saffron whacked Violet's arm angrily, and the apple fell to the floor.

"Saffron! Smarten up!"

She burst into noisy tears. "I hate you! I want to go home!"

"Right," Violet said. "Too bad we don't have one."

"Violet!" I glared at her and raised my voice over Saffron's angry sobs. "Like that's going to help. She's *five*, all right? Give her a break."

Violet looked like she might start crying too. "You think it's easy being the oldest, Wolf? Because guess what. It isn't. Actually, it sucks."

"But at least you—"

"No, listen. You think I don't feel like I'm abandoning you all? That I don't feel totally guilty about it?"

"So don't do it," I said. "You do have a choice, you know."

We stared at each other for a moment, Saffron screaming her head off, half the Walmart shoppers of Nelson staring at us. Violet ran her hands through her hair. "God, I hate my life," she said.

Ty was practically sprinting back toward us, Whisper bouncing up and down on his back with each stride. "Got it!" He waved a piece of paper at us. "Okay, so call your grandmother already. Let's get out of here before we get kicked out."

Violet took the paper from him, stuck some coins in the phone and dialed. Ty and I watched, holding our breath. Even Saffron seemed to realize that this phone call was important and switched off the waterworks. Thank god, because that noise in the background would hardly endear us to our grandmother. *Their* grandmother, I reminded myself. Not mine.

"Hello," Violet said. "Um. Is this Diane Brooks? Um. This is Violet. Your granddaughter." She looked at me and mouthed, *It's her.* "Well, actually, we're right here in Nelson…Well, me and the twins, and Wolf. Jade's son… No, my dad isn't with us." She bit her lip, listening. "Right.

He's in Chilliwack, actually. Yeah, with Jade…On the Greyhound. We just arrived…"

She met my eyes and held up crossed fingers.

I crossed mine too.

"It's kind of a long story," Violet said. "But we're at the Walmart, and we were kind of hoping we could come and stay with you. Just for a few days."

My heart was racing. What were we going to do if she said no? We didn't have much money left, and we had nowhere else to go. Saffron looked at me and held up her crossed fingers, and I wondered how much she and Whisper understood about what was going on.

This whole idea had been completely crazy. Irresponsible. A thousand times worse than what my mom had done—at least she'd always made sure we had enough to eat and a tent to sleep in and a van that sort of worked. At least she'd had a plan.

"We're really tired," Violet said. "And the twins are hungry. Could you come and get us? And we can explain it all when we see you?" Her voice wobbled. "*Please*?"

She listened for a few seconds, nodding to us while she did. "Okay. We'll be right out in front of the Walmart. See you soon. Thank you…um, thank you, Grandma."

She hung up the phone. "She'll be here in ten minutes."

"Did she sound mad?" I asked.

Violet made a face. "She didn't exactly sound thrilled."

"I guess it's probably a bit of a shock," I said. "Us just showing up like this. Without our parents and everything."

"Well, she's coming to get us," Violet said. "So that's something anyway."

"I hope she has ice cream," Saffron said.

"Me too," I said. "Me too."

Twenty-Eight

I DIDN'T KNOW what to expect this grandmother to be like. It was weird to think she was Curtis's mother. Actually, it was weird to think Curtis even *had* a mother. Curtis and my mom had been together for over six years, but he hadn't lived with us all the time, and he was away a lot, doing different jobs here and there—tree planting up north or working on fishing boats for months at a time. In some ways, I didn't feel like I knew him all that well. He'd never wanted me to call him Dad or anything like that. Not that I wanted to, exactly, but it was weird being the only one who didn't.

Violet had said *Grandma* when she was on the phone, and I wondered if the twins would call her that too, and what I should call her. Diane? Mrs. Brooks?

Maybe I'd just avoid calling her anything.

We stood in front of the Walmart, waiting. Violet bit her nails. "I hope she's not too mad," she said.

"Why would she be mad?" Saffron asked.

"She won't be," I said, glaring at Violet over Saffy's head. "She'll be happy to see you."

Saffron put her hands on her hips. "Then why did Violet say she'd be mad?"

I could see Whisper listening carefully to every word. The last thing we needed was for her to be in full meltdown mode when her grandmother drove up. Time for a distraction. "Hey," I said loudly, "let's all guess what color her car will be. I say white…"

Ty caught on. "Black."

"Pink," Saffron decided.

"How about you, Whisper? Blue? Green?" I paused. "Brown?"

"Red," Whisper said.

It was so quiet—and so unexpected—that I almost missed it. I swallowed and tried to stay calm. I didn't want to freak her out or make a huge deal of it. "Red, huh? You're guessing red? Okay."

Saffron didn't seem to notice anything unusual, but Violet was staring at Whisper like she had suddenly grown a second head or something. I shook my head at her warningly. "How about you, Vi? What color is her car going to be?"

"Um, right. Blue. Did someone already say blue?"

"Nope. Okay, so…" I broke off. "Is that her?"

A dark-red SUV was slowing down and pulling over to the curb in front of us. I squinted but couldn't really see through the tinted windows.

Violet blew out a long breath. "Red," she said. "You win, Whisper."

Whisper grinned.

"Pink would look *much* nicer," Saffron said.

We all stared as the driver got out and walked around the front of the car. "Violet?" she said. "I wouldn't have recognized you."

I wouldn't have recognized her either, not from the grandmother image in my head. She looked more like a Diane Brooks than a grandmother. She didn't seem very old, for one thing. Her brown hair was glossy and kind of stylish, with frosty-blond highlights, and she was wearing a purple skirt with a black jacket. She had lots of bracelets on both arms, and they jangled when she moved her hands.

"Hi," Violet said. I'd never heard her sound so shy before. "Um, this is Ty. My boyfriend. And—"

"And Saffron and Juniper." She turned to the twins. "Well, you've certainly grown."

She said it kind of disapprovingly, like she'd rather they hadn't. I exchanged looks with Violet.

"Yes?" Saffron said, her voice rising as if it was a question. Whisper looked down at the ground.

"Thanks for coming to pick us up, Mrs. Brooks," I said. "Um, I'm Wolf."

"Of course. You wouldn't remember me, but I did meet you a few times on Lasqueti Island, when Curtis started spending time with Jade. Your mother. Before I left." She looked me up and down with that same critical frown. "You used to be a tiny little thing."

I nodded politely. "Violet told me you lived there for a while."

"A year, yes. But I've been here in Nelson for a long time. I'm in real estate now." She turned back to Violet. "What are you all doing here? I had no idea you were coming. I haven't spoken to Curtis for a couple of years. Not since that time he came out here when the twins were toddlers."

Violet stuck out her lower lip and blew a long noisy breath that lifted her bangs off her forehead. "It's a super-long story."

"Hmm." Mrs. Brooks gave her a skeptical look and then gestured to the car. "Well, get in. You can tell me about it on the way."

Violet did most of the talking. She started with my bee project, explaining how I'd done all this research on why bees were dying and all that stuff. She didn't make it sound like the trip was all my fault this time. She explained how Jade had latched on to the subject and started her own website about it, and how things had kind of spiraled from there— the trip and George the van and leaving school early and Ty not being allowed to come.

Mrs. Brooks interrupted her a couple of times to clarify some point, but mostly she just drove and listened, even though Violet didn't seem to be getting anywhere close to explaining why we had all appeared, without warning and without our parents, at the Walmart in Nelson.

Violet had just gotten to the part where we did our first presentation in Vancouver when Mrs. Brooks held up a hand to indicate she should stop. "This is my place," she said, pulling into the driveway beside a meticulously landscaped front yard. "So Violet, just pause the story there and let's get you all settled in with a drink and something to eat—I bet you haven't had dinner, have you? And then you can tell me the rest."

Violet nodded, looking relieved. I wondered if she'd been planning to leave out the part where she took off with Ty. It wasn't really relevant, but so far she'd included every last detail, right down to which exams she was missing and the specific design of the twins' costumes. As we got out of the car, she grabbed my shoulder. "Do you think it's going well?" she whispered.

"It's hard to tell. Did you know she hadn't talked to Curtis in years?"

"Sort of. I knew they had a big fight and that was why she left Lasqueti. And I knew it didn't go well when he visited with the twins. I think he was hoping to fix things, but it didn't work out." She made a face. "I can't stop babbling—I'm so nervous."

I leaned close, my mouth inches from her ear. "You're going to tell her about Whisper, right? About her not talking and everything?"

"Of course. That's mostly why we're here, right?"

I nodded. "Yeah. But don't explain that part in front of the twins."

She pulled back and gave me a scornful look. "Give me some credit. I'm not a complete idiot, Wolf."

Twenty-Nine

WE ALL TROOPED into the house after Mrs. Brooks. It was nice, but in a super-tidy way that made it look like no one actually lived there. Polished wood floors, mostly covered by beige carpeting. A glass coffee table with a vase of flowers on it. An enormous L-shaped couch—white leather, with a few brown polka-dot cushions placed at strategic intervals. A big television but no books, no magazines, no games, no empty coffee mugs.

I stood there awkwardly while Violet followed her grandmother into the kitchen to help get drinks and food for everyone. Ty plunked himself down on the living room couch, shoving a polka-dot cushion aside, and after a moment's hesitation I flopped down beside him. The twins trailed into the room behind us. They looked tired and pale, and Saffy had awful dark circles under her eyes.

"You guys hungry?" Ty asked them.

Whisper nodded and snuggled up beside me, her head on my shoulder. She felt warm, and her hair was sticking damply to her forehead.

Saffron climbed onto Ty's lap. "Tell us a story about Buzzy."

Ty's eyes met mine. "I'm all storied out, kiddo."

"Please?"

"Got no more in me right now, Saffy. Seriously. Maybe at bedtime, okay? After we have something to eat." Ty leaned his head back on the couch cushions, eyes closed.

"I'll tell you a story," I said.

Both girls turned to look at me, Whisper smiling, Saffron unconvinced.

"Um, so there was once a little monkey—" I began.

"A bee," Saffy said.

"No, Buzzy is Ty's story," I said.

"Tell a story about George then."

"George the van?"

She nodded.

I sighed. "Fine. Once upon a time there was a van called George. George was black and yellow, and he had stripes like a bee. And more than anything, George wanted to…" I hesitated, trying to think of something a van might want.

"To fly," Whisper breathed.

"Okay." My breath caught in my throat. She was speaking. That was twice she'd spoken today. Did that mean I hadn't made things worse, at least? "More than anything," I said, "George wanted to fly."

Saffron giggled. "A flying van!"

"That's right. Because the thing about George…" I paused, thinking, looking down at Whisper. A hint of a smile flickered at the corners of her mouth. "The thing about George," I went on, "was that he didn't know he was a van. He thought he was a bee. But all the other bees he saw were so much smaller and fuzzier than him, and they all knew how to fly…"

Whisper's eyes closed. Saffron leaned her head on Ty's chest, listening.

"George watched the bees flying around. He watched them landing on the bright flowers and gathering pollen, and he wondered why he was stuck on the ground. He wondered where his wings were and when he would be able to fly." I had a lump in my throat all of a sudden, and I found myself blinking back tears. What the hell was wrong with me? Practically crying over a stupid imaginary van. "Um, so one day he met a…um, he met a…"

"A skateboard," Ty said.

I rolled my eyes. "Fine, a skateboard. And the skateboard couldn't fly either."

Violet walked in, carrying a tray. She put it down carefully on the coffee table in front of us: a plate of cheese and crackers, some cut-up apples, a package of chocolate-covered cookies.

"You want some food?" I asked.

Saffron shook her head drowsily. "More story."

Whisper didn't answer. She was already fast asleep.

I sighed. Time to come up with a happy ending. "Okay. So George and the skateboard started to talk…"

Violet gave me a funny look, but I shrugged and plowed on. "And the skateboard said, 'Hey, you have wheels like I do. So maybe you're not a bee. Maybe you're a skateboard.' But George was pretty sure he wasn't a skateboard." I waited, watching Saffron. Her eyes were closed and her mouth slightly open. "Saffy?" No answer.

"Out cold," Ty said. He shifted Saffron off his lap. "Here, there's room for them both if we move."

We eased the girls down so that they were lying with their heads together in the middle of the couch and their bare feet—very dirty bare feet—at the ends. I sat down on the carpet and grabbed a cracker and a thick slice of pale yellow cheese. "So where's your grandmother?" I asked in a low voice. "What did she say?"

"Take a wild guess," she said flatly. "Take a wild guess what she's doing right now."

I shook my head. "What?" I stared at her, too tired to play games. "Isn't she going to help us? To help Whisper?"

"She's on the phone to Curtis," Violet said wearily.

"Oh." I chewed, swallowed. "You explained about Whisper not talking and needing help? And Mom not getting it and just making things worse?"

"I explained everything." Violet shrugged. "I don't know what I expected. I should have known she wouldn't do anything."

"Maybe she'll explain," I said. "Maybe Mom and Curtis will listen to her."

"Maybe," Violet said. "But I wouldn't count on it."

We all sat there in silence for a long moment. I watched the twins asleep on the couch, their hair tangled and their faces flushed.

"What do you want to do, Violet?" Ty asked softly. "Your dad and Jade…I know the van's not going, but they'll probably catch a bus and come, right? You want to take off before they get here?"

Violet burst into tears and ran from the room. I heard the front door open and then bang closed. Ty sighed, stood up and followed her. I just sat there, waiting. Eating cheese and crackers. Thinking. Was Ty right that our parents would come? Or would Mom insist on sticking to their schedule? She had rescheduled all that stuff in Hope and Kamloops and Kelowna. And she'd been prepared to leave Vancouver without Violet if necessary.

"Well, it looks like we should get those two to bed."

I looked up. Mrs. Brooks was standing in the doorway with her hands on her hips. I hastily swallowed a mouthful of too-dry cracker. "Um. Yeah. They kind of crashed."

"No doubt," she said. "Where's Violet?"

"She's with Ty," I said. "Outside, I think."

"Is she?" She studied me for a long moment. "Well. You certainly look like your mother."

"I guess," I said. Something about her tone of voice made me think this was not a compliment.

"Follow me," she ordered. "I'll show you where you'll be sleeping."

I cleared my throat. "Did you talk to our parents?"

"I talked to Curtis," she said.

"What did he say?"

"He said they'll catch the next bus, which isn't until the morning. They'll be here tomorrow night."

"Both of them?" I held my breath.

"I assume so," she said.

I was trying very hard not to assume anything at all.

Mrs. Brooks had a spare room with a queen bed for the twins, and she'd put a thin foam mattress on the floor for me. White sheets and a navy-blue comforter were neatly folded at the end of it.

"What about Violet and Ty?" I asked.

"Ty can sleep in the living room," she said. She was out of breath from carrying Whisper up the stairs. "On the couch. And I've put an air mattress in my office for Violet."

We pulled the covers back and laid Saffron and Whisper down, hair and teeth unbrushed and clothes still on. They didn't even stir. Their feet looked filthy against the clean white sheets, and I quickly pulled a blanket up over them, hoping Mrs. Brooks hadn't noticed.

"I guess I'll go to bed now too," I said. I wasn't sleepy exactly; I just wanted to be by myself.

"Of course," Mrs. Brooks said. "I'll see you in the morning."

After she'd gone back downstairs, I took a towel from the pile she'd left us and folded it in a double layer underneath Whisper's bum, just in case she wet the bed. And then I lay down on my own bed and tried to relax. I couldn't stop thinking though. They weren't even real thoughts— just jumbled bits and pieces of thoughts, like my brain was randomly skipping ahead and going back over everything that had happened over the last few days. Vi saying she was going away with Ty. Hazel and Tess playing Monopoly with me. Anna's story about the war. George, the van who couldn't fly.

Mom telling me I had to be a warrior...

Next thing I knew, the sun was streaming in the window and Whisper was sitting up in bed, staring down at me.

MRS. BROOKS MADE breakfast for us all: toast, jam, scrambled eggs, sliced-up apples and cheese, and the kind of orange juice you make from frozen concentrate and that has that weird taste. Once Duncan and I ate a whole can of it frozen, like ice cream. Or more like sorbet, I guess. It tasted okay that way—super sweet—but I didn't like how it tasted as juice. Mom doesn't buy juice much—she says water's better for you—but when she does, it's the made-from-real-fruit stuff.

Mrs. Brooks didn't say anything about her conversation with Curtis or about what we'd done, taking off on our parents. It felt weird not talking about it—kind of like there was this great big ugly *thing* sitting in the middle of the table between the butter dish and the stacks of toast, and we were all pretending it wasn't there.

"Pass the jam, Wolf?" Violet said.

I picked it up and handed it across the table to her.

"Thanks."

Long awkward silence.

"Can I have more toast with peanut butter?" Saffron asked.

"Here, Saf," Ty said. "I'll make you one." He picked up a piece of toast and started spreading peanut butter on it.

More awkward silence. I could hear the knife scraping on the toast and the too-loud sound of my own chewing. Ty passed Saffron the toast. Whisper nibbled on a slice of apple. Violet met my eyes across the table, and I wondered what she was thinking. I hadn't talked to her since she'd run out of the room in tears the night before.

"Well," Mrs. Brooks said. "When you've all finished eating, perhaps you could watch the twins, Tyler? I'd like to have a talk with Violet and Wolf."

Apparently we weren't going to ignore that big ugly thing in the middle of the table after all.

Half an hour later, Ty was playing with Saffron and Whisper in the backyard, and Vi and I were sitting in the living room with Mrs. Brooks.

"Thanks for doing the dishes," she said. She was sitting on a straight-backed wooden chair, her ankles crossed. Even though we weren't going anywhere, just sitting in her own house, she was wearing dark-beige tights and pointy-toed shoes with high heels.

Vi and I were side by side on the couch. It was low and squishy, which meant we had to look up to meet her eyes. "Sure," I said. I cleared my throat. "Um, thanks for breakfast."

Mrs. Brooks ignored me and looked straight at Violet. "Your father will be here this evening," she said.

Violet nodded. "I know," she said. "You told me last night."

"Me too," I said, feeling left out. "You told me too."

"I assume they'll want to continue this trip," she said.

"Well, we can't just go back," Violet said. "It's not that easy. We moved out of our place. Our stuff's all in storage..."

"What about Whisper?" I interrupted. "That's the main reason we came here. To get someone to help Whisper."

Mrs. Brooks shook her head. "You need to talk about this with them," she said. "Not with me. Really, it has absolutely nothing to do with me."

"I've tried," I said hopelessly. "You don't understand. My mom...She's really, really, *really* single-minded about the bees."

"Oh, I've met your mother, Wolf," she said. "Believe me, I understand more than you think."

Her voice was so dry and so bitter that I actually flinched. "Well...but if you understand...then can't you..." I trailed off. Because I didn't think she understood anything at all. She just didn't *like* my mother.

Mrs. Brooks leaned toward me. "Whether or not I agree with her choices, Jade is still Whisper's mother," she said. "And Curtis is her father. And what they do is none of my business. As, I might add, they have made quite clear in the past."

"But don't you think Whisper needs help?"

She sighed. "I think it's quite possible that she does. But I'm afraid that what I think is irrelevant."

"But they'll listen to you." Violet inched forward, perching on the edge of the couch with her elbows on her knees, hands pressed together under her chin like she was praying. "If you tell them—"

Mrs. Brooks gave a harsh laugh. "Like you listen to your parents, Violet?" She shook her head, uncrossed her ankles and leaned back. "Curtis hasn't listened to me since he was, oh, about eight years old. And I'm not part of his life anymore. He's made that clear."

"Won't you even *try*?" I said.

She shook her head. "Whisper seems perfectly healthy," she said. "They're not hitting her or starving her or neglecting her, are they?"

I couldn't believe she had to ask. "They're not hurting her," I said. "Not physically. Of course they aren't. I mean, they love her. But she isn't talking, and dragging her off on this trip is just making her worse."

"That's right," Violet said. "She hasn't spoken—well, hardly at all—since we left."

"But it's not a new problem, her being anxious," Mrs. Brooks pointed out. "I remember when Curtis brought them to meet me before, they were just three, and Jade had taken them out of preschool because Whisper wasn't talking and seemed like she just wasn't ready." She looked from Violet to me and back to Violet. "I think you both need to think really hard about this."

"We have been thinking about it," I burst out. "I've been thinking about it all the time."

She nodded. "Because it's easier to worry about Whisper than about the things Jade is saying."

"What?" I stared at her. "No. That's not—"

She kept going. "It's easier to worry about Whisper than admit you don't want to dress up as a bee and be paraded around in front of strangers."

I turned to Violet. "You told her I didn't want to dress up?"

"Well, so what? It's true. You didn't want to," Violet said defensively.

"But it's not the point," I said. "It's—"

Mrs. Brooks interrupted me. "And Violet. You were upset about missing school—"

"I never said I wasn't," Violet said. "The whole trip was a stupid idea. So what?"

I folded my arms across my stomach, which was starting to hurt. "All that stuff—that's not why we came here. That's got nothing to do with it."

Mrs. Brooks looked at me, her eyebrows raised. "Are you sure about that, Wolf? And you, Violet? Are you sure you aren't both using Whisper as an excuse to run away?"

We both stared back at her. I couldn't believe how much she was missing the point.

"I suggest you think about it," she said. "And think about what it is you're running away from. Think about what it is you really need to say to your parents." She stood up and walked out of the room.

Violet and I sat there in silence, staring after her as she disappeared into the kitchen and banged the door closed behind her.

There was a buzzing in my ears that sounded like a million bees.

Violet looked at me. "She totally doesn't get it. I should've known she wouldn't."

"She just doesn't like Mom," I said. "It's obvious."

"I don't think she likes Curtis much either," Violet said. "He always said she was super controlling and interfering."

"You're just bringing this up now?" I stared at her. "It was your idea to come here. Anyway, that doesn't even make sense. We *want* her to interfere, and she won't."

Violet shrugged. "Didn't have anywhere else to go, did we? And she *is* Whisper's grandmother. You'd think she'd care a bit."

"Yeah." I scowled. "Instead, she's acting like Whisper's fine and we're just using her as an excuse to complain about stuff."

"Maybe she's right," Violet said. "I mean, it's not *just* about Whisper, is it?"

"So it sucks for all of us. What difference does it make?" I clenched my hands into fists and pressed them against my thighs.

"None, I guess. If she won't help, there's nothing else we can do."

"We can try to talk to them," I said. "Mom and Curtis, when they get here. We have to make them *listen*, right? Not let Mom brush it off or change the subject…"

"You can try."

"*We* can try," I said. "Both of us."

"Not me," Violet said. "I told you. Ty and I are going to take off before they get here."

"You can't. I need you to help."

"I'm sorry." She looked like she might cry. "I'm really sorry, Wolf."

She wasn't going to change her mind. I could see it in her eyes and the way she was clenching her jaw so tightly. I closed my eyes for a minute and let out a long shaky breath I hadn't realized I'd been holding. "I'll miss you," I said.

"You'll be okay."

"I guess." I didn't even know what *okay* meant. Everything beyond right now was a great big blank. "Are you going to Calgary? How will you get there? You don't have any money."

"This friend, this guy Ty knows…He's driving from Vancouver to Calgary. Like, right now. Ty talked to him last night." She pulled her phone out of her pocket and checked her messages. "So, yeah. He's two hours away from Nelson. He's going to pick us up this afternoon."

"And that's that. You're just going to leave." I met her eyes. "Aren't you scared at all?"

"Don't worry about me," she said. "I'll be fine."

And I knew she would. Violet might technically be only fifteen, but she was a very grown-up fifteen. Plus she was the kind of person who always took care of herself. You could call it selfish, I guess, but it wasn't totally a bad thing.

Anyway, she'd be with Ty.

I was more worried about myself.

Thirty-One

THE TWINS WERE playing in the yard. Ty had made some soapy liquid from water and dish soap, and twisted bits of wire into loops, and the three of them were blowing bubbles. I lay back on the grass and watched the bubbles shimmer and float away, climbing high into the blue sky and disappearing out of sight.

I couldn't do it. I couldn't spend the next few weeks—months, maybe—crammed in that stinky van, looking after the twins, watching Mom do presentation after presentation and thinking about the bees dying and disappearing and what it would mean for the world. For the future.

I didn't agree with Violet that Mom was nuts. Single-minded, maybe, but she was right about the bees needing to be saved, and, like Eva said, it took people with passion to make real change. Lots of people just ignored problems, or else they worried and complained instead of actually doing anything. Mom wasn't like that. I thought it was cool that she was putting all her energy into the one thing she felt mattered the most.

But I wished what mattered the most to her was us. Her family. Me.

Of course, I knew she'd say that we *were* what mattered most. That we were the reason she was doing all this—she loved us and wanted us to have a future.

I heard Duncan's voice in my head: *That blog of your mom's? That's some pretty crazy stuff.*

Was he right? Or was Mom right, and everyone else was in denial? I didn't know what to think about that or how I was supposed to feel. But back on the bus, when Violet had said that thing about *needing* to run away, it hit me like a punch to the guts.

I felt the same way. I sat up and watched Saffron and Whisper giggling and running, chasing after bubbles that reflected every color of the rainbow. I couldn't imagine leaving them, even if I had somewhere to go.

Which I didn't.

Unless...I stood up and headed back inside. Violet was lying on the couch, watching TV, and didn't even look up when I walked past. I went into the kitchen, closed the door behind me and picked up the black cordless phone.

I dialed the only number I knew by heart: Duncan's.

Duncan and I had been friends for three years. He lived with his mom, Alexa. It was just the two of them, so their place had always seemed really small and quiet compared to mine. Alexa was nice. She'd gone back to school to do social work a year ago, so she studied a lot, and they didn't have much money, but I knew she liked me. They always invited me over, and one time Alexa said to me, in this very serious voice, "*Wolf, if you ever need—well, anything, really—you know you can talk to me, right?*"

I'd just said, *Yeah, sure, of course.* I'd been kind of embarrassed and couldn't imagine what I'd want to talk to her about. But now I wondered…what if I needed a place to stay?

The phone rang and rang, and my hands were suddenly sweaty on the receiver.

No one answered. Finally, after about eight rings, there was a click and a recorded voice—Duncan's mom's: "Hi, you've reached Alexa and Duncan. Leave a message if you want to, and we'll call you back."

"Hi," I said. I hated leaving messages, but Duncan really hated it when people hung up. *Dude, I have enough hang-ups already,* he'd told me once. "It's me," I said. "Wolf. Um, I was—"

There was another click, and then a voice cut me off midsentence. "Wolf! It's me, I'm here. I was just in the middle of something on my computer, and I figured it'd be for my mom so I didn't bother…Anyway. So."

"Hi," I said again.

"Where the photon are you?"

"Nelson," I said. "We're in Nelson."

"That's, like, a hippie town, right?"

"I dunno," I said. "All I've seen is the Walmart. Anyway, we're at Vi's grandmother's place now. And…uh, things have been kind of complicated." It was hard to know where to begin. "Listen, Dunc. Uh, you think there's any chance I could stay with you guys for a bit?"

"Totally," he said. "Awesome."

"Ask your mom, okay?"

"She's out. But she'll say yes. For sure. She likes you." He laughed. "She'd trade me in for you, dude. She totally would. She thinks you're *sweet*."

"Sweet?"

"Yeah. That's what she always says. *That Wolf just seems like such a* sweet *boy…*"

I cut him off. "Yeah, all right. Jeez."

He laughed again. "I miss you, dude. It'd be one hundred percent awesome to have you stay with us."

"Thanks."

There was a pause, and then Duncan said, "So…what's up? Trip not working out for you?"

My throat got all tight again, and I had to clear my throat so my voice wouldn't come out in a squeak. "Not so well," I said. "Uh, you know Whisper?"

"Your sister."

"Yeah. She's, like, not really talking. And…" Mrs. Brooks was right, I thought. It wasn't just about Whisper. "This whole thing, you know, about the bees. It's…I dunno. It's just kind of…" I trailed off.

"Dude, tell me about it. Waaayyy out there."

"I dunno," I said again. "I mean, it really is serious, what's happening to the bees. It really is a big problem. I get that."

"Sure, yeah. I mean, that's why you did that project, right? I remember it, dude. It was awesome. All that stuff about pesticides and commercial beekeeping. Like how they artificially inseminate the queen bees. Freaky stuff."

Duncan had helped me figure out how to make the website for my bee project. I'd even credited him on the site: *Tech Support—Duncan Collins*. "Yeah," I said. "So I'm not, like, dismissing it or anything." I cleared my throat again and gripped the phone tighter in my hand. I felt sort of disloyal, saying what was in my mind. "But this trip…It's just…It's kind of…"

"It's pretty whack," Duncan said. "Like, extreme. Katie was really worried. She kept asking me if I thought you were all right with all that stuff on your mom's website."

"Did she?" I missed Katie. "I mean, it's okay if my mom wants to do this. Maybe it'll even make a difference. I dunno. But—"

"But you don't want to do it," Duncan finished for me.

"That's right," I said. "I don't."

Saying it out loud felt like taking off a heavy sweater on a hot day. Or opening the window in the stinky van and letting cool, fresh air blow in.

"Well, no kidding," Duncan said. "'Course you don't."

"So you'll talk to your mom?"

"Yeah. But I can tell you with one hundred percent certainty that the answer will be yes."

Mrs. Brooks made lunch—cheese sandwiches and slices of cantaloupe and a pitcher of iced tea—and carried it all out to a picnic table in the backyard. The twins were already out there, sort of helping but mostly getting in the way.

"Tell Violet and Ty that lunch is ready, would you, Wolf?" she said.

I went back into the house. Violet and Ty had been on the couch, watching TV, the last time I saw them, but they weren't there anymore. "Vi?" I called out.

No answer.

I ran upstairs to the office, where she'd slept the night before, to see if her stuff was still there, but I already knew.

She was gone.

I kneeled down on the floor, staring at the deflated air mattress and the neatly folded blankets. Everything was blurry. I brushed away my tears angrily and clenched my hands into tight fists, pounding them against my thighs.

There was a great big hollow space inside my chest. A great big empty *aching* space.

I couldn't believe she hadn't even said goodbye.

I told Mrs. Brooks that Violet and Ty had gone for a walk. I didn't know if she believed me, but she didn't say anything— just raised her eyebrows and handed me a plate of food.

"Thanks," I said. I couldn't meet her eyes. I felt bad about lying to her, but if I told her they'd gone, she'd get upset. I figured it was better just to leave that one until Mom and Curtis got here. Even if I told Mrs. Brooks now, it wasn't like she'd be able to do anything about it.

"Grandma," Saffron said, "Whisper doesn't eat these things."

Mrs. Brooks raised her eyebrows. "What things, Saffron?"

"*These* things." Saffron gestured at their plates. "She only eats orange cheese. This is yellow cheese."

I looked at Whisper. She was licking a slice of melon, over and over. Just licking it like it was a Popsicle. "It's fine," I said. "Whisper's trying."

"You let me know if you want something else, Whisper," Mrs. Brooks said.

Apparently she didn't believe us about Whisper not talking. I took a bite of my sandwich and thought about Violet.

I wasn't worried about her.

I was too angry to worry.

In a few hours, Curtis and Mom would arrive—and it would be up to me to make them understand.

Thirty-Two

TIME WAS WEIRD that afternoon, both too fast and too slow. I played with the twins—drawing pictures for them to color, making up George the Van stories and suffering through at least a dozen games of Crazy Eights, which was torturous as neither of them could stand to lose. I was getting more and more anxious.

Mrs. Brooks fussed about the house, trying to decide where Curtis and Mom could sleep and wondering aloud where on earth Violet and Ty had got to. Finally, she said she was off to the bus station to pick up our parents. "I do wish your sister hadn't wandered off. Very inconsiderate of her." She draped a silky scarf around her neck. "Please keep an eye on your sisters until I get back with your mother and Curtis."

I put down my cards. "Yes. I will. We'll be fine." It was what was going to happen after they all got back that I was worried about.

"It's your *go!*" Saffron said, nudging me hard with her elbow.

"Right. Right." I watched Mrs. Brooks leave and had a sudden urge to take off myself. Just get up and walk out that door and start to run. But it didn't make sense to run away when we'd already *run* away…I swallowed, took a deep breath and played a card. "Saffy, pick up two."

She scowled. "You always make *me* pick up."

"Because you go after me, dummy. I can't make Whisper pick up."

"Don't call me dummy." She picked up two cards.

"Sorry," I said.

Saffron slapped down a Jack. "Miss a turn, Whisper!"

Whisper's bottom lip trembled.

"Look, how about we play something else?" I suggested. "Or watch some TV? Or—"

"No," Saffron said. "Crazy Eights."

I looked at Whisper. She held up her cards and nodded, which I took to mean she wanted to keep playing. "Fine," I said. "Then no getting upset, okay?"

Two identical shrugs.

"Okay?" I said again. "Because one more meltdown and I quit. For real this time."

Two matching nods.

I thought of Duncan and his mom, and their cozy little apartment. But even if Mom agreed, which seemed unlikely, how could I leave the twins? Who would look after them while Mom did her presentations? Because no matter how much Mom and Curtis loved them—and I knew they loved them tons—they weren't always good at figuring out that sort of thing.

Like Mom always said, they were big-picture people. Sometimes they forgot about taking care of the details.

Forty minutes later, I heard the scrunch of tires in the gravel driveway. "They're here," I said, getting to my feet.

Whisper clapped her hands together, and Saffron ran to the door and threw it open.

"Saffy!" Mom's voice, high and anxious. "My sweet little kitten, come here." And then she was inside, sweeping Saffron into her arms and lifting her off the ground.

Whisper clutched my hand and pushed her face against my leg.

I bent down to her. "Are you feeling shy? It's okay. Go on."

Mom looked over at us. "Whisper, love. My little bug. Come here, honey."

And Whisper let go of my leg and dashed across the living room to Mom. I stood there awkwardly. I could hear Curtis just outside the door, talking to Mrs. Brooks, but I couldn't make out what he was saying. I wasn't looking forward to telling him that Violet had left.

Mom was crying, kneeling on the floor with her arms around the twins, stroking their hair. "I was so worried."

"They're fine, Mom," I said. She was going to get them all upset if she kept that up. "They've had a nice visit with their grandmother, and they're just fine. There's nothing to worry about."

She glared at me, but I guess she took the hint, because she got to her feet. She cleared her throat, and when she spoke, her voice had dropped an octave. "Of course they are," she said. "I just missed my little bugs."

Those crazy, mixed-up feelings were boiling up inside me again, and I had to dig my nails into my palms to distract myself.

Curtis and Mrs. Brooks walked into the room. Curtis put one arm around Mom's waist and tousled Whisper's hair with his other hand. He nodded at me. "Wolf."

"Hi," I said. *Now what*, I thought. My heart was beating so fast and hard I could actually feel it in my head, a thumping pressure inside my ears. Whatever was going to happen next, I just wanted to get it over with.

"Well," Mrs. Brooks said. "Perhaps Saffron and Whisper should play upstairs in their room while you three visit. And Violet...Wolf, is she still not here?"

I shook my head. "She won't be," I said.

Mom looked at me sharply. "What do you mean?"

I gestured to the twins with my chin. I didn't want to talk in front of them.

"Come on, you two." Mrs. Brooks held out a hand toward them. "Let's get you a snack to take up with you. Or maybe you could help me make some cookies. What do you think?"

At least she seemed to be getting fond of the twins. She was actually smiling at them—not a fake smile but a warm one, like she really meant it. "I thought chocolate chip," she said, "but you can help me take a look in my recipe book…"

"Wolf. What do you mean, *she won't be*?" Mom said again. Her voice was sharp-edged and loud, and Saffron and Whisper squirmed out of her grasp and followed Mrs. Brooks into the kitchen. The door closed behind them.

And it was just Mom and Curtis and me standing there in the living room.

Showtime, I thought. But I didn't have a show prepared. I didn't have a bunch of balls to juggle to represent Vi and me and the twins, to show what a mess Mom's ideas and this crazy trip were making of our lives. I wasn't a performer.

"Sit down," Curtis said, pointing at the couch.

I sat.

He didn't. He stood there, towering over me. "Where. Is. Violet?"

"She and Ty left this afternoon," I said. "With a friend of Ty's. They're going to Calgary."

"Calgary!"

"She'll be okay," I said. "She'll probably call you when she gets there."

Mom dropped onto the couch beside me and held her head in her hands. "What a mess."

"And you just let her go?" Curtis was shouting now. "You just let her leave?"

I stared at him. "It's not like I could stop her." I raised my voice. "It's not like she even said goodbye! What was I supposed to do?"

"Don't shout at Wolf," Mom said. "It's not his fault."

Curtis shook his head and swore softly under his breath. "That girl. That girl. She's impossible."

"She'll be okay," I said again. There weren't many things I felt certain about, but that was one of them. Violet did what she needed to do. She was a fighter.

"Wolf, what on earth were you all thinking? Why did you all run away like this? Did something happen?" Mom's forehead was creased, one hand twisting in her long hair.

"Nothing happened," I said. "We just couldn't keep doing it."

"Doing what?" She put her hand on my knee and squeezed. "Tell me."

I swallowed hard, trying to find the right words. "Pretending," I said.

"Pretending? What do you mean?"

"Acting like everything's okay. Like all we care about is saving the bees."

She shook her head. "I don't understand."

"I'm trying to explain!" It came out as a shout. "You just don't ever listen. I've been trying to tell you forever."

"I'm listening now," she said. "So tell me. What is going on?"

"Well…" I lowered my voice. "For one thing, in case you haven't noticed, Whisper isn't talking. Like, at all." I suddenly remembered that she'd spoken yesterday—twice—but decided not to confuse matters by bringing that up now. "And she's always having these meltdowns and stuff."

"You think I don't know that?" Mom said. "You think I don't worry about her?"

"I've tried to talk to you about it," I said. "You just brush it off and say she's fine. But she isn't fine. She's not even close to fine. She worries about stuff all the time, until her stomach hurts. And she wets her bed, and now she doesn't even talk."

"Wolf. I'm her *mother*. I'm well aware of her struggles."

"So why do you just brush it off when I try to talk to you? Why do you pretend nothing's wrong?"

She took her hand off my knee and leaned away from me. "Maybe I just don't think it's something you need to be worrying about."

"Right," I said. "Because I should just be worrying about the bees dying and the world ending. Because that's THE ONLY THING THAT MATTERS!" I was shouting again, but I didn't care. "You don't care that Violet's messed up her tenth-grade year, or that she's in love with Ty, or that I'd rather be back at school with Duncan, or that Whisper's scared all the time. All you care about are the STUPID BEES!"

Mom blinked like I had slapped her, and her cheeks flushed a blotchy red. "That's not true, Wolf. That's not true at all."

"It might as well be," I said. "Because that's how you act. Ignoring what we want, dragging us off on this trip, acting like it isn't making everything worse."

Mom's eyes were shining with tears. "Wolf. Wolf. The whole reason we're doing this—the reason I care about the bees so much—is because I want there to be a future for all of—"

"DON'T!" I yelled. "Don't say that! Don't say you're doing this for us."

She stopped. "Then I don't know what to say. Because that is the truth."

There was a long silence. I didn't know what to say either. It seemed like this was what it always came back to: Mom being so focused on the bees that she couldn't see anything else. The conversation Violet and I had had on the bus came back to me: *How do you plan for the future when your own parents don't believe you have one?*

I couldn't make my mom trust in the future no matter how much I wanted her to.

Thirty-Three

I SAT THERE beside my mom, staring at my bare feet on the beige carpet. I didn't have any words, but my mind was full of thoughts, all buzzing this way and that like a hive full of bees. Though that didn't make sense, because my thoughts were all over the place, going around in useless circles. Chaotic. And bees were anything *but* chaotic.

Bees had their own rules, and they followed them. That was why it was so disturbing—so wrong—when they suddenly disappeared by the thousands, flying away from their hives and disappearing, abandoning their young…

I caught my breath. "Mom. Bees never abandon their young, right? Not normally?"

She frowned. "Of course not."

"And that's why—like, with colony collapse disorder— it's so weird when they do that, right? When they leave the young and just vanish?"

"Right." She frowned. "Wolf, what are you getting at?"

"Just…when bees do it, it's like it's a sign that things are messed up, right? That the balance is off?"

"Right. So?"

I curled my toes, dug my fingernails into my palms and took a deep breath. She had to understand. I had to *make* her understand. "So a family is kind of like a colony, right? And ours…well, I guess it's sort of collapsing. I mean, Violet's run away, Whisper's not talking, and I'm—well, I hate it. I hate what we're doing. This trip. Thinking all the time about what a mess the world is. It's like *our* balance is off. And…" I caught my breath, wished Violet was beside me, forced myself to keep going. "I know you love us, okay, Mom? And I know you don't mean to abandon us. But that's kind of how it feels."

Mom had tears in her eyes. I wanted to take it all back, to make it seem like everything was okay. But I couldn't. Because it was true. Every last word of it.

"Wolf. Wolf." She pulled me toward her, her hands in my hair. "Why didn't you say something?"

I squirmed free. I didn't want her petting me. I wanted her to understand that loving us wasn't enough. Love wasn't magic, and it wasn't going to fix everything. "I tried!" I said. "I tried. Like, a thousand times! And you never listened."

"Did Violet feel…does she feel the same way?" Curtis got off his chair, moved across the room and perched beside us on the arm of the couch. "I know she wanted to be with Ty, but when we said he could come with us, I thought she was happy. I thought that was the end of it."

"You should talk to her," I said. "But yeah, she's tired of the bee thing taking over our lives. And she's worried about Whisper too."

"We've all been worried about Whisper," Curtis put in. "She's always been an anxious kid."

I looked at him and shrugged. "You don't do anything about it."

"What exactly do you think we should be doing?" Mom said. "Dragging her from doctor to doctor? Getting her labeled as having some kind of disorder? Put on medication?" She shook her head. "I'm not convinced that's the way to go."

"But you're not an expert," I said. "So maybe you should at least talk to someone who is."

"I've looked it up online," Mom said. "The not-talking thing. It's called selective mutism. And it's related to anxiety." She looked at me. "But I'd rather let her grow and learn in her own way, without labels. Without pressure."

I snorted. "Not much pressure, feeling like it's up to us to save the world."

Mom looked stricken. "Oh, Wolf. No. No. I've never said that. I just think we should all contribute what we can."

I made a face. "We're not all like you. And what you're asking Whisper to do—the presentations, dressing up, talking to people we don't even know…" I trailed off. "It's too much. It's way, way too much for Whisper."

She opened her mouth, then closed it again. Bit her lip. Leaned toward me. "And you, Wolf?"

"Yeah," I said, and my voice cracked a little. It was starting to do that lately. "For me too."

"Oh, Wolf," she said again. "My poor, brave Wolf."

She looked like she might start to cry. I dropped my gaze to the floor and felt like a turtle pulling its head inside its shell. "I spoke to Duncan," I said stiffly. "I can stay with him and his mom for the summer. While you guys do this trip."

She hesitated. "Let us talk about it, okay? I have to think about the twins too. Without Violet and you to help out... I don't know how this is going to work."

Not my problem, I told myself. I imagined the shell around me, hard and tough. Imagined her words bouncing off it, not touching me. "Is the van fixed?" I asked.

Curtis shook his head. "Piece of crap, that van."

Found On Road Dead, Violet had said. Seemed like she hadn't been so far off. Though maybe it was the vegetable-oil conversion that had messed things up. Curtis was pretty handy, but he wasn't actually a mechanic. Plus he got most of the vegetable oil from fast-food places and Chinese restaurants. Maybe the engine was gummed up with stray pieces of egg roll. That'd explain the rancid smell.

Curtis stood up. "Wolf, how about you take the girls outside? Your mom and I need to talk. And I need to talk to my mother." He shook his head. "Still can't believe you all just turned up on her doorstep. Must have given her quite a shock."

"Uh-huh." I hesitated. "Um, she said she hadn't talked to you for a couple of years."

He met my eyes. "Yeah. Well, she and your mom never got along."

"So now it's all my mom's fault that you guys don't talk?" I said. "That's not very fair."

Mom didn't look mad though. She just rolled her eyes. "It sure wasn't easy, when she was on Lasqueti. Didn't matter what I did, it wasn't good enough. According to Diane, I'm the reason her son dropped out of college. Never mind that I didn't even *meet* him until two years after that."

Curtis shook his head but said nothing.

Mom snorted. "She's impossible."

Curtis put a hand on my mom's knee. "Wolf, I'm not blaming your mom. My mother and I had problems way before I met Jade. Since I was your age. She's the kind of person who wants everything to be a certain way. Like, it's her way or the highway, you know? So she wasn't ever an easy person to get along with. Let alone live with."

Mom leaned toward him, and when she spoke her voice was wobbly. "I suspect Wolf might say the same about me."

I looked at her, startled. "Yeah. But, uh, it's okay. Mom. You know."

She put her arms around me and gave me a quick, hard hug. "I know. And I love you." Then she let me go, leaned back and studied my face like she'd never seen it before. "Growing up so fast."

I felt heat flare in my cheeks and looked away. My face was probably bright red. "Um, I'll go get the girls then. So you guys can talk." I got up, walked into the kitchen and pressed my cool hands to my cheeks. Saffron and Whisper were eating chocolate chips while Mrs. Brooks beat eggs in a blue pottery bowl.

"Saffy? Whisper? You guys want to come outside and play?"

"Is Mom still here?" Saffron asked. She looked apprehensive, her speech too quick, her eyes a little too wide.

"Yeah, don't worry. She and Curtis want to talk to your grandmother." I stole a chocolate chip from the mound on the counter in front of her. "Come on."

Saffy batted my hand away. "Hey!"

I laughed.

Whisper slid a chocolate chip from her pile toward me. "Here," she said, ever so softly.

"Thanks, kiddo." I ruffled her hair. "You two really need a bath, you know that?"

"You said we could play," Saffron said, dashing for the door to the yard.

I started to follow her, then turned back. "Thanks, Mrs. Brooks." I thought about what Curtis had said, about how it must have been a shock for her to have five kids suddenly show up on her doorstep. "Um, for everything. For taking care of us and everything."

"You're a good big brother, Wolf." She washed her hands at the sink and dried them on a dish towel. "Go play with your sisters. And try not to worry. Things have a way of working themselves out."

Whisper's hand found mine and squeezed. I looked down at her. "Come on," I said. "Let's go play."

Thirty-Four

MOM AND CURTIS and Mrs. Brooks talked for a really long time. I played with the twins until the sun was low in the sky and our shadows stretched long across the lawn, and then I took them inside and up to bed.

"Are Mom and Dad staying here too?" Saffron asked.

I tucked the covers up to her chin and tight around her shoulders, the way she liked. "Tonight, yeah. You'll see them in the morning."

"What about George?"

"Well, George still needs a bit of fixing," I told her.

"Not the real George," she said. "A George story. Tell us a George story."

I sighed. "Really?"

"Yeah. Please?"

I looked sideways at Whisper, snuggled up on the other side of the bed. "You want a George story too?"

She nodded.

I brushed her hair off her forehead. "Let me think a minute. And make some room. Push over." I lay down between them, wriggling exaggeratedly to make space for myself while they giggled. "Okay," I began. "Once there was a van called George. He wasn't a very big van, and sometimes he got scared of things."

"What kind of things?" Saffron asked.

"Well, he was scared of loud horns. He was scared of driving over something sharp and getting a flat tire. He was scared of big trucks and noisy highways. He was scared of squirrels and cats. And, most of all, he was scared of..." I paused and poked them both in the ribs. "...little girls."

Whisper giggled.

"Why little girls?" Saffron asked.

I shook my head. "He didn't know why. He just was. Sometimes being scared is like that." I looked at them. "Right?"

They both nodded solemnly.

"So one day, George was sitting in the driveway and two little girls came running toward him. He was so scared his wheels trembled, and his exhaust pipe shook. But guess what?"

"What?"

"Well, those two little girls painted him new and shiny. They told him that they were his friends. And George realized that they weren't so scary after all...And, uh, that's the end."

"That's *it*?" Saffron made a disgusted face. "That was a *terrible* story."

"Sorry. I'm tired. Best I could do."

"*Humph.*" She scowled. "You can't just end a story like that, before it's properly over."

"It's just over for right now," I told her. "There'll be lots more George stories." I kissed the top of her head and then the top of Whisper's head. "I'll see you two in the morning. Night."

"Night," Saffron said.

"Night," Whisper breathed, ever so quietly.

Down in the living room, the three grown-ups were still deep in conversation. When I walked into the room, there was a sudden hush.

"Um, I guess you're still talking," I said.

"It's okay." Mom shifted to one side and patted an empty spot on the couch, between her and Curtis. "Come sit."

I did. "I told the girls you'd still be here in the morning."

"Of course we will." She looked at me. "I probably don't tell you this often enough, but Curtis and I really do appreciate everything you do for the twins."

"He's a good big brother," Mrs. Brooks said approvingly.

For some reason, it rubbed me the wrong way. Like they were all leading me somewhere I might not want to go. I shrugged and looked down at the floor. "Um. Yeah, okay."

Curtis shifted to face me. "We need to make some decisions."

"Uh-huh." I waited.

"First, about Whisper," Mom said. "We weren't ignoring her needs, you know. We honestly thought being out of school, being with family all day…we thought that would be good for her."

"Yeah. Not so much," I said.

"Maybe," Mom said. "Though I do wonder if she might just be adjusting to a big transition. Perhaps, if we kept going, she would settle into this new routine and things would improve."

I nodded. "She said good night to me just now. Out loud. Well, not *loud*, but you know what I mean."

"Did she?"

"Yeah. But Mom, she shouldn't have to wear a costume if she doesn't want to, and I don't think she should have to help with the presentations either. It's not fair to make her. She's five."

"She just looks so darn cute in it."

Mrs. Brooks sighed audibly. She didn't quite roll her eyes, but you could tell she wanted to.

"Not if she's screaming until she's blue in the face," I said. "That's less cute. Anyway, the bees are your thing. I think if you want to do it, that's cool, but I don't think you should make us do it."

"I thought you cared about the bees," she said. "I thought you understood how important this is."

I hesitated. "I do care about what happens to the bees. Of course I do."

"But?"

"I don't know. I don't want to wear a costume. But I could…maybe Duncan and I could develop my website or something. You know?" I pictured Duncan's fingers flying over the keys, working his magic. "Like, we could use my research and stuff, but make it interactive. Facts and quizzes and links to videos…I bet Duncan could even make a game with bees as a theme. Like a *Save the Bees* game. And we could link it to your website. That'd help, right?"

Curtis gave an appreciative nod. "Good thinking."

"Have you talked about me staying with him?" I asked.

"Yes." Mom squeezed my knee. "You know I'm very fond of Duncan."

My heart sank. "But?"

"We don't want to just abandon the trip." She saw me open my mouth, about to protest, and held up a hand, palm out toward me. "Wait. Let me finish."

I nodded.

"You know how much work it has been, planning this. And maybe we were too ambitious. Maybe we need to scale it back." She looked at Curtis and then back at me. "We can't do it without you. Not look after the girls and do the presentations."

"Yeah." I'd already figured that out.

"So here's what we're thinking. The van—we'll get it running again, but I don't think it'll make it across Canada, to be honest. So we're thinking…just British Columbia. Two months, max. We'd be back in Victoria for school in September."

Curtis leaned forward. "My mother's offered to look after you and the twins, if you want. Or you could go stay with Duncan, and the twins could stay here with their grandmother. But"—he held up a finger—"if the girls aren't comfortable with that…if they want to stay with your mom and me…"

I finished his sentence. "Then you'll need me to come with you."

"Yes. We will," he said.

"Fine." It wasn't though. My heart was beating really hard, and that crazy rage feeling was building up inside me again. They were acting like this was some big compromise when this whole trip was only supposed to be for the summer anyway. What difference did it make if we drove to Quebec or just drove around BC? It would still be a nightmare. The girls shouldn't get dumped for a whole summer with a grandmother they barely knew. And I wasn't going to spend two months looking after them, listening to my mom predict the end of the world as we knew it.

I turned back to my mother. "No," I said. "It's not fine. It's not even a little bit fine."

She and Curtis exchanged glances. "Wolf. Be reasonable," she said.

"I'm *tired* of being reasonable," I said. "I can't believe you'd even consider just leaving the twins here. You just said Whisper's anxious, and now you're talking about abandoning her. Just leaving them with someone they don't even know."

"No one is abandoning anyone," Mom snapped.

I didn't say anything. Mrs. Brooks stood up and smoothed her skirt, her bracelets jangling. "I think I'm going to excuse myself," she said. "I'll see you in the morning."

We all watched her leave. You could tell from the way she held her shoulders, all tight and twitchy, that I had offended her.

Curtis sighed. "Well. What are you suggesting, Wolf?" He leaned toward me. "You think we should just go home and go back to our regular lives? Forget about the bees? Is that what you want? Huh? You want us to pretend that the world isn't heading into a major catastrophe?"

He was jabbing at me with his words, like a kid poking a turtle with a stick. I shrugged, keeping my head in my imaginary shell, trying not to react to his goading. Trying to think. "A week," I said finally. "I'll look after the twins for one week. Not all of BC. Just the Okanagan. Short drives, a few presentations." I folded my arms across my chest. "And I'm not dressing up. And I don't think the twins should have to either."

"A week," she repeated. "And then what?"

"Then we all go home," I said. "Or I go to stay with Duncan, and you figure out how to manage." I looked at Curtis. "I don't see why you can't look after the twins anyway. It's not like you even do anything in the presentation."

There was a long, long silence. Curtis pulled his eyebrows so low they practically met in the middle, and two deep creases bracketed his mouth. Mom was twisting the end of her braid between her fingers and blinking back tears. None of this had turned out how she'd imagined it, I thought.

I remembered how hard she'd worked, getting everything ready for the trip—the website, the costumes, the juggling show, the flyers, the van—and for a moment I felt so bad, so selfish, I could hardly stand it.

But I couldn't back down.

"If we go home, I can finish school," I said. "And…well, maybe Violet and Ty would come back. If they had some-where to come back to."

"A week," Mom said again. She brushed the back of her hand across her eyes. Then, surprising me, she started to laugh. "My little bees are more like little rosebushes. You all just want to put down roots."

I didn't say anything, but I didn't think I had much in common with bees or rosebushes. "Does that mean we can go home?" I said. "Just one week and then we can go home?"

She looked at Curtis and then back at me. "Yes," she said. "Yes, okay. One week, and we'll go home."

"We'll figure out some other way to do this," I said. "Save the bees, I mean. Going home doesn't mean we have to give up. We can write letters; we can organize all kinds of stuff. Duncan and I, we'll do stuff online. And I can do more, later on, when I finish school." Maybe I'd even become a scientist, I thought. Maybe I'd find out what was killing the bees and save them for real. Or maybe I'd do something entirely different, like studying distant galaxies.

I couldn't make my mom trust in the future, but she couldn't stop me believing I had one. I knew I did.

"I spent my whole life in one ghastly suburb," Mom said. "Until I was almost twenty. And all I wanted was to pull up my roots and get away. To be free to travel and explore and not be tied down and stuck in a place full of mindless consumers. I wanted to make a difference in the world, you know?"

I nodded. "I want to make a difference too, Mom. I just want to do it in my own way."

"You will," she said. She put an arm around me and pulled me in for a hug. "You already do, Wolf. You make the world better just by being here."

Upstairs, the twins were fast asleep. Whisper had pulled the blankets right over her head, and when I folded them back, her face was flushed and her hair sweaty. Bath tomorrow, for sure.

I switched off the light, stripped down to my undies and T-shirt and snuggled into my own bed on the floor. There was pale moonlight streaming in through a gap in the thin curtains, and my sheets smelled fresh and clean, like fabric softener. I stretched my legs out, enjoying the coolness of the sheets, and wondered where Violet was sleeping tonight. I wished I could talk to her. And I wondered what Saffron and Whisper would say about all our plans when we told them in the morning. If they'd be happy to stay with their grandmother or if they'd want to go with Mom and Curtis. And George the Van, of course…

I really hoped I could go to Duncan's, but either way, I thought, it'd be okay.

I'd be okay.

Last fall there was this weird thing that happened not too far from where we lived. This family—tourists from the States, I think, with a couple of little kids—got lost in a corn maze and couldn't find the exit. It was pretty huge, and they ended up going around in circles, getting more and more desperate, getting hungry and scared and practically freezing in the maze all night long, until the farmer saw their car sitting in the parking lot the next morning and realized they were still in there.

Anyway, when I looked back at the last few months—since I did my bee project and Mom started planning the trip—it sort of felt like that. Like we were lost in our own crazy maze. I think I'd almost forgotten there was a whole big world outside the maze—a world where most people weren't obsessed with this one thing. A world full of people who believed that there was a future, who didn't think bees dying meant the world was ending, who didn't talk about *these last doomed years.*

A world full of people who saw a future.

And right now, lying here in the moonlit darkness, I felt oddly hopeful for the first time in ages. Just knowing that there was a whole world outside the maze made it all more bearable. It gave me hope.

And that made all the difference.

Acknowledgments

MANY THANKS TO all the wonderful people who helped me to write this book: my partner, Cheryl; my son, Kai; my parents, Ilse and Giles; my coffee-shop writing buddies, Kari and Alex; my always-inspiring students; and my editor and friend Sarah Harvey. Thanks also to everyone at Orca—I couldn't ask for a better team to work with.

ROBIN STEVENSON is the author of numerous
books for kids and teens. Her previous middle-grade
novel, *Record Breaker*, won the 2014 Silver Birch Award
and was a finalist for a BC Book Prize. Robin lives on the
west coast of Canada with her partner, son and two cats—
an elderly one-eyed pirate cat called Noah and a floppy,
purring heap of fluff called Mojang. Robin sometimes
edits books and teaches creative writing, and she always
loves hearing from readers. For more information, visit
www.robinstevenson.com.